WACKY
WEDNESDAY

By

Dr. Seuss

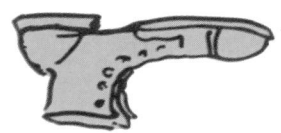

WACKY
WEDNESDAY

By
Dr. Seuss

writing as
Theo. LeSieg

Illustrated by George Booth

HarperCollins *Children's Books*

™ & © Dr. Seuss Enterprises, L.P.
All Rights Reserved

A CIP catalogue record for this title is available from the
British Library.
No part of this publication may be reproduced, stored
in a retrieval system or transmitted in any from or by
any means, electronic, mechanical, photocopying,
recording or otherwise, without the prior permission of
HarperCollins Publishers Ltd, 1 London Bridge Street
London SE1 9GF

3 5 7 9 10 8 6 4

ISBN 978-0-00-82 3996-1

© 1974 by Dr. Seuss Enterprises, L.P.
All Rights Reserved
Illustrations © 1974 by Random House Inc.
Published by arrangement with Random House Inc.,
New York, USA
First published in the UK 1975
This edition published in the UK 2017 by
HarperCollins *Children's Books,*
a division of HarperCollins*Publishers* Ltd
1 London Bridge Street
London SE1 9GF

www.harpercollins.co.uk

Printed and bound in India by Replika Press Pvt. Ltd.

It all began
with that shoe on the wall.
A shoe on a wall . . . ?
Shouldn't be there at all!

Then I
looked up.
And I said,
"Oh, MAN!"

And that's how
Wacky Wednesday
began.

I looked out
the window.
And I said,
"GEE!"

More things were wacky!
And I saw three.

I went
down the hall
and I said,
"HEY!"

Three
more things
were wacky today!

In the
bathroom,
MORE!

In the
bathroom,
FOUR!

I began to dress.
Then I said,
"WOW!"

Four MORE things
were wacky now!

I looked
in the kitchen.
I said,
"By cracky!
Five more things
are very wacky!"

I was late for school.

I started along.

And I saw that

six more things were wrong.

And then seven more!

And the Sutherland sisters!
They looked wacky, too.

They said,
"Nothing is wacky
around here but you!"

"But look!" I yelled.
"Eight things are wrong
here at school."

"Nothing is wrong,"
they said.
"Don't be a fool."

ABCDEFGHIJKLMNOP
QRSTUVWXZY

$1+2=3$

I ran into school.

I yelled to Miss Bass . . .

... "Look!
Nine things
are wacky
right here
in your class!"

"Nothing is wacky
here in my class!
Get out!
You're the wacky one!
OUT!"
said Miss Bass.

I went out
the school door.
Things were worse than before.
I couldn't believe it.
Ten wacky things more!

FOUR SALE

Then I
counted
ELEVEN!

Then . . .
twelve WORSE things!
I got scared.
And I ran.

I ran
and knocked over
Patrolman McGann.

"I'm sorry, Patrolman."
That's all I could say.

"Don't be sorry," he smiled.
"It's that kind of a day.
But be glad!
Wacky Wednesday
will soon go away!"

"Only twenty things more
will be wacky," he said.

"Just find them
and then
you can go
back to bed."

Wacky Wednesday was gone
when I counted them all.
And I even got rid
of that shoe on the wall.

FOX IN SOCKS

BY

Dr. Seuss

TICK

HarperCollins *Children's Books*

For
Mitzi Long and Audrey Dimond
of the
Mt. Soledad Lingual Laboratories

The Cat in the Hat
™ & © Dr. Seuss Enterprises, L.P. 1957
All Rights Reserved

3 5 7 9 10 8 6 4

ISBN 978-0-00-820150-0

© 1965, 1993 by Dr. Seuss Enterprises, L.P.
All Rights Reserved
A Beginner Book Published by arrangement with
Random House Inc., New York, USA
First published in the UK 1966
This edition published in the UK 2016 by
HarperCollins Children's Books,
a division of HarperCollins Publishers Ltd
1 London Bridge Street
London SE1 9GF

Visit our website at:
www.harpercollins.co.uk

Printed and bound in India by Replika Press Pvt. Ltd.

Fox in Socks

Fox

Socks

Box

Knox

3

Knox in box.
Fox in socks.

Knox on fox
in socks in box.

Socks on Knox
and Knox in box.

Fox in socks
on box on Knox.

Chicks with bricks come.
Chicks with blocks come.
Chicks with bricks and
blocks and clocks come.

Look, sir. Look, sir.
Mr. Knox, sir.
Let's do tricks with
bricks and blocks, sir.
Let's do tricks with
chicks and clocks, sir.

First, I'll make a
quick trick brick stack.
Then I'll make a
quick trick block stack.

You can make a
quick trick chick stack.
You can make a
quick trick clock stack.

11

And here's a
new trick, Mr. Knox. . . .
Socks on chicks
and chicks on fox.
Fox on clocks
on bricks and blocks.
Bricks and blocks
on Knox on box.

13

Now we come to
ticks and tocks, sir.
Try to say this
Mr. Knox, sir. . . .

14

Clocks on fox tick.
Clocks on Knox tock.
Six sick bricks tick.
Six sick chicks tock.

Please, sir. I don't
like this trick, sir.
My tongue isn't
quick or slick, sir.
I get all those
ticks and clocks, sir,
mixed up with the
chicks and tocks, sir.
I can't do it, Mr. Fox, sir.

I'm so sorry,
Mr. Knox, sir.

17

Here's an easy
game to play.
Here's an easy
thing to say. . . .

New socks.
Two socks.
Whose socks?
Sue's socks.

20

Who sews whose socks?
Sue sews Sue's socks.

Who sees who sew
whose new socks, sir?
You see Sue sew
Sue's new socks, sir.

That's not easy,
Mr. Fox, sir.

Who comes? . . .
Crow comes.
Slow Joe Crow comes.

Who sews crow's clothes?
Sue sews crow's clothes.
Slow Joe Crow
sews whose clothes?
Sue's clothes.

Sue sews socks of
fox in socks now.

Slow Joe Crow sews
Knox in box now.

Sue sews rose
on Slow Joe Crow's clothes.
Fox sews hose
on Slow Joe Crow's nose.

Hose goes.
Rose grows.
Nose hose goes some.
Crow's rose grows some.

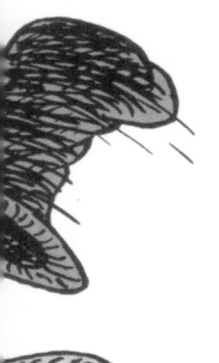

Mr. Fox!
I hate this game, sir.
This game makes
my tongue quite lame, sir.

Mr. Knox, sir,
what a shame, sir.

We'll find something
new to do now.
Here is lots of
new blue goo now.
New goo. Blue goo.
Gooey. Gooey.
Blue goo. New goo.
Gluey. Gluey.

Gooey goo
for chewy chewing!
That's what that
Goo-Goose is doing.
Do you choose to
chew goo, too, sir?
If, sir, you, sir,
choose to chew, sir,
with the Goo-Goose,
chew, sir. Do, sir.

Mr. Fox, sir,
I won't do it.
I can't say it.
I won't chew it.

Very well, sir.
Step this way.
We'll find another
game to play.

Bim comes.
Ben comes.
Bim brings Ben broom.
Ben brings Bim broom.

Ben bends Bim's broom.
Bim bends Ben's broom.
Bim's bends.
Ben's bends.
Ben's bent broom breaks.
Bim's bent broom breaks.

Ben's band. Bim's band.
Big bands. Pig bands.

BOOM

Bim and Ben lead
bands with brooms.
Ben's band bangs
and Bim's band booms.

Pig band! Boom band!
Big band! Broom band!
My poor mouth can't
say that. No, sir.
My poor mouth is
much too slow, sir.

Well then . . .
bring your mouth this way.
I'll find it something
it can say.

Luke Luck likes lakes.
Luke's duck likes lakes.
Luke Luck licks lakes.
Luke's duck licks lakes.

Duck takes licks
in lakes Luke Luck likes.
Luke Luck takes licks
in lakes duck likes.

I can't blab
such blibber blubber!
My tongue isn't
made of rubber.

Mr. Knox. Now
come now. Come now.
You don't have to
be so dumb now. . . .

Try to say this,
Mr. Knox, please. . . .

Through three cheese trees
three free fleas flew.
While these fleas flew,
freezy breeze blew.
Freezy breeze made
these three trees freeze.
Freezy trees made
these trees' cheese freeze.
That's what made these
three free fleas sneeze.

Stop it! Stop it!
That's enough, sir.
I can't say
such silly stuff, sir.

Very well, then,
Mr. Knox, sir.

Let's have a little talk
about tweetle beetles. . . .

What do you know
about tweetle beetles?
Well . . .

When tweetle beetles fight,
it's called
a tweetle beetle battle.

And when they
battle in a puddle,
it's a tweetle
beetle puddle battle.

AND when tweetle beetles
battle with paddles in a puddle,
they call it a tweetle
beetle puddle paddle battle.
AND . . .

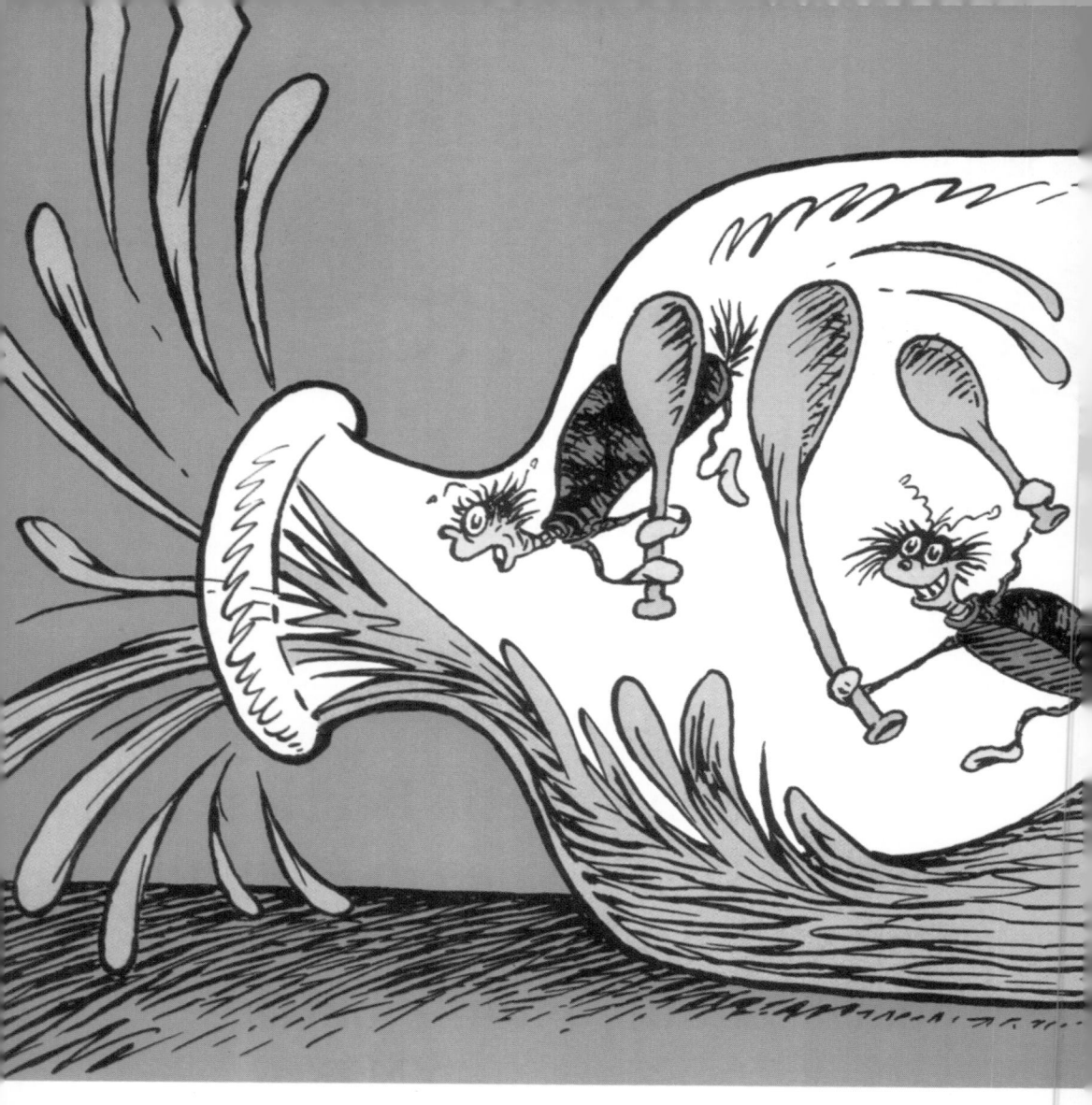

When beetles battle beetles
in a puddle paddle battle
and the beetle battle puddle
is a puddle in a bottle . . .

52

. . . they call this
a tweetle beetle
bottle puddle
paddle battle muddle.

AND . . .

53

When beetles
fight these battles
in a bottle
with their paddles
and the bottle's
on a poodle
and the poodle's
eating noodles . . .

. . . they call this
a muddle puddle
tweetle poodle
beetle noodle
bottle paddle battle.

AND . . .

55

Now wait
a minute,
Mr. Socks Fox!

When a fox is
in the bottle where
the tweetle beetles battle
with their paddles
in a puddle on a
noodle-eating poodle,
THIS is what they call . . .

58

. . . a tweetle beetle
noodle poodle bottled
paddled muddled duddled
fuddled wuddled
fox in socks, sir!

Fox in socks,
our game is done, sir.
Thank you for
a lot of fun, sir.

OH, THE PLACES YOU'LL GO!

YOU'LL GO!

By

Dr. Seuss

HarperCollins *Children's Books*

5 7 9 10 8 6

ISBN 978-0-00-820148-7

© 1990 by Dr. Seuss Enterprises, L.P.
All Rights Reserved
Published by arrangement with
Random House Inc., New York, USA
First published in the UK 1990
This edition published in the UK 2016 by
HarperCollins *Children's Books,*
a division of HarperCollins*Publishers* Ltd
1 London Bridge Street
London SE1 9GF

The HarperCollins website address is:
www.harpercollins.co.uk

Printed and bound in India by Replika Press Pvt. Ltd.

Congratulations!
Today is your day.
You're off to Great Places!
You're off and away!

You have brains in your head.
You have feet in your shoes.
You can steer yourself
any direction you choose.
You're on your own. And you know what you know.
And *YOU* are the guy who'll decide where to go.

You'll look up and down streets. Look 'em over with care.
About some you will say, "I don't choose to go there."
With your head full of brains and your shoes full of feet,
you're too smart to go down any not-so-good street.

And you may not find *any*
you'll want to go down.
In that case, of course,
you'll head straight out of town.

It's opener there
in the wide open air.

Out there things can happen
and frequently do
to people as brainy
and footsy as you.

And when things start to happen,
don't worry. Don't stew.
Just go right along.
You'll start happening too.

OH!
THE PLACES YOU'LL GO!

You'll be on your way up!
You'll be seeing great sights!
You'll join the high fliers
who soar to high heights.

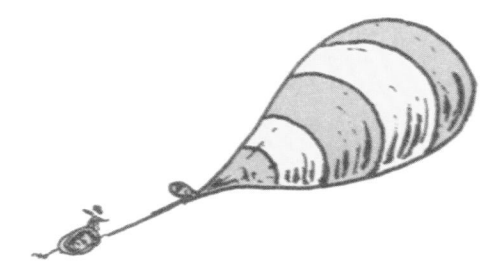

You won't lag behind, because you'll have the speed.
You'll pass the whole gang and you'll soon take the lead.
Wherever you fly, you'll be best of the best.
Wherever you go, you will top all the rest.

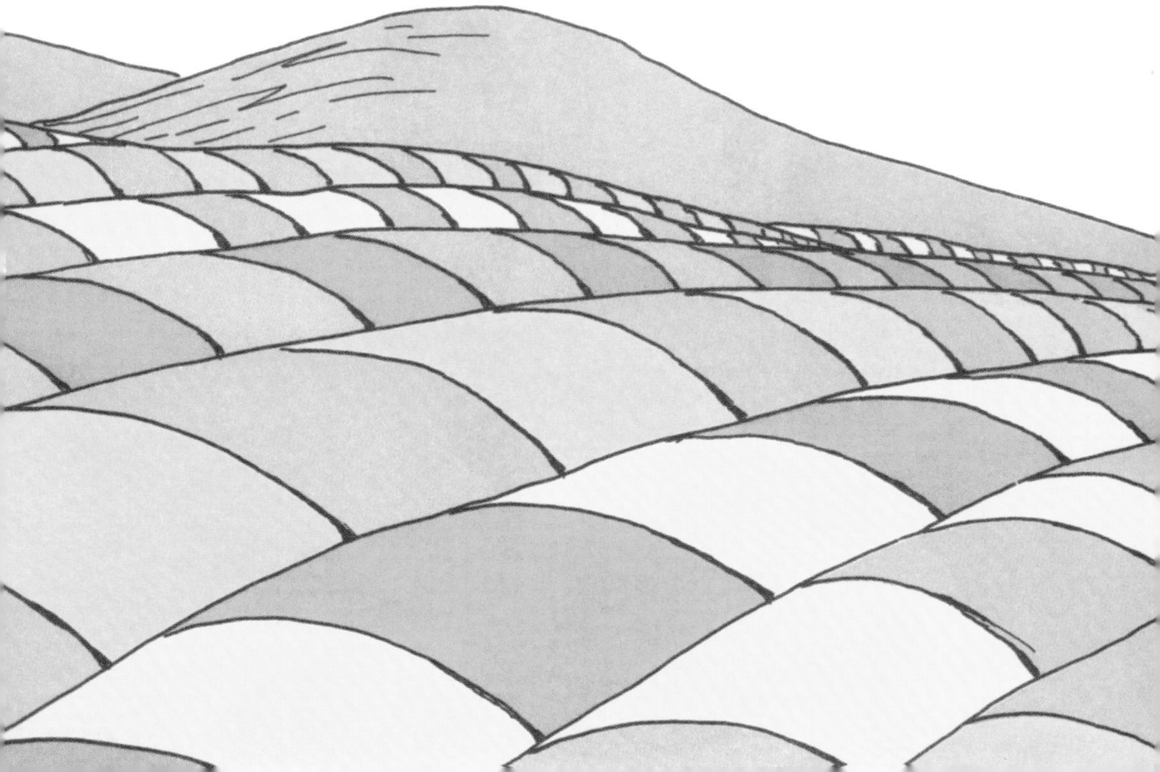

Except when you *don't*.
Because, sometimes, you *won't*.

I'm sorry to say so
but, sadly, it's true
that Bang-ups
and Hang-ups
can happen to you.

You can get all hung up
in a prickle-ly perch.
And your gang will fly on.
You'll be left in a Lurch.

You'll come down from the Lurch
with an unpleasant bump.
And the chances are, then,
that you'll be in a Slump.

And when you're in a Slump,
you're not in for much fun.
Un-slumping yourself
is not easily done.

You will come to a place where the streets are not marked.
Some windows are lighted. But mostly they're darked.
A place you could sprain both your elbow and chin!
Do you dare to stay out? Do you dare to go in?
How much can you lose? How much can you win?

And *IF* you go in, should you turn left or right . . .
or right-and-three-quarters? Or, maybe, not quite?
Or go around back and sneak in from behind?
Simple it's not, I'm afraid you will find,
for a mind-maker-upper to make up his mind.

You can get so confused
that you'll start in to race
down long wiggled roads at a break-necking pace
and grind on for miles across weirdish wild space,
headed, I fear, toward a most useless place.

The Waiting Place . . .

. . . for people just waiting.
   Waiting for a train to go
   or a bus to come, or a plane to go
   or the mail to come, or the rain to go
   or the phone to ring, or the snow to snow
   or waiting around for a Yes or No
   or waiting for their hair to grow.
   Everyone is just waiting.

Waiting for the fish to bite
or waiting for wind to fly a kite
or waiting around for Friday night
or waiting, perhaps, for their Uncle Jake
or a pot to boil, or a Better Break
or a string of pearls, or a pair of pants
or a wig with curls, or Another Chance.
Everyone is just waiting.

NO!
That's not for you!

Somehow you'll escape
all that waiting and staying.
You'll find the bright places
where Boom Bands are playing.

With banner flip-flapping,
once more you'll ride high!
Ready for anything under the sky.
Ready because you're that kind of a guy!

Oh, the places you'll go! There is fun to be done!
There are points to be scored. There are games to be won.
And the magical things you can do with that ball
will make you the winning-est winner of all.
Fame! You'll be famous as famous can be,
with the whole wide world watching you win on TV.

Except when they *don't*.
Because, sometimes, they *won't*.

I'm afraid that *some* times
you'll play lonely games too.
Games you can't win
'cause you'll play against you.

All Alone!
Whether you like it or not,
Alone will be something
you'll be quite a lot.

And when you're alone, there's a very good chance
you'll meet things that scare you right out of your pants.
There are some, down the road between hither and yon,
that can scare you so much you won't want to go on.

But on you will go
though the weather be foul.
On you will go
though your enemies prowl.
On you will go
though the Hakken-Kraks howl.
Onward up many
a frightening creek,
though your arms may get sore
and your sneakers may leak.

On and on you will hike.
And I know you'll hike far
and face up to your problems
whatever they are.

You'll get mixed up, of course,
as you already know.
You'll get mixed up
with many strange birds as you go.
So be sure when you step.
Step with care and great tact
and remember that Life's
a Great Balancing Act.
Just never forget to be dexterous and deft.
And *never* mix up your right foot with your left.

And will you succeed?
Yes! You will, indeed!
(98 and¾ per cent guaranteed.)

KID, YOU'LL MOVE MOUNTAINS!

So . . .
be your name Buxbaum or Bixby or Bray
or Mordecai Ali Van Allen O'Shea,
you're off to Great Places!
Today is your day!
Your mountain is waiting.
So . . . *get on your way!*

THE SNEETCHES
AND OTHER STORIES

By

Dr. Seuss

HarperCollins *Children's Books*

™ & © Dr. Seuss Enterprises, L.P.
All Rights Reserved

3 5 7 9 10 8 6 4

ISBN 978-0-00-824004-2

Published by arrangement with
Random House Inc., New York, USA
First published in the UK in 1965
This edition published in the UK 2017 by
HarperCollins *Children's Books,*
a division of HarperCollins*Publishers* Ltd
1 London Bridge Street
London SE1 9GF

www.harpercollins.co.uk

Printed and bound in India by Replika Press Pvt. Ltd.

MIX
Paper from
responsible sources
FSC® C016779

This book is produced from independently certified FSC® paper
to ensure responsible forest management.

Now, the Star-Belly Sneetches
Had bellies with stars.
The Plain-Belly Sneetches
Had none upon thars.

Those stars weren't so big. They were really so small
You might think such a thing wouldn't matter at all.

But, because they had stars, all the Star-Belly Sneetches
Would brag, "We're the best kind of Sneetch on the beaches."
With their snoots in the air, they would sniff and they'd snort
"We'll have nothing to do with the Plain-Belly sort!"
And whenever they met some, when they were out walking,
They'd saunter straight past them without even talking.

When the Star-Belly children went out to play ball,
Could a Plain Belly get in the game. . .? Not at all.
You only could play if your bellies had stars
And the Plain-Belly children had none upon thars.

When the Star-Belly Sneetches had frankfurter roasts
Or picnics or parties or marshmallow toasts,
They never invited the Plain-Belly Sneetches.
They left them out cold, in the dark of the beaches.
They kept them away. Never let them come near.
And that's how they treated them year after year.

Then ONE day, it seems . . . while the Plain-Belly Sneetches
Were moping and doping alone on the beaches,
Just sitting there wishing their bellies had stars . . .
A stranger zipped up in the strangest of cars!

"My friends," he announced in a voice clear and keen,
"My name is Sylvester McMonkey McBean.
And I've heard of your troubles. I've heard you're unhappy.
But I can fix that. I'm the Fix-it-Up Chappie.
I've come here to help you. I have what you need.
And my prices are low. And I work at great speed.
And my work is one hundred per cent guaranteed!"

Then, quickly, Sylvester McMonkey McBean
Put together a very peculiar machine.
And he said, "You want stars like a Star-Belly Sneetch . . . ?
My friends, you can have them for three dollars each!"

"Just pay me your money and hop right aboard!"
So they clambered inside. Then the big machine roared
And it klonked. And it bonked. And it jerked. And it berked
And it bopped them about. But the thing really worked!
When the Plain-Belly Sneetches popped out, they had stars!
They actually did. They had stars upon thars!

Then they yelled at the ones who had stars at the start,
"We're exactly like you! You can't tell us apart.
We're all just the same, now, you snooty old smarties!
And now we can go to your frankfurter parties."

"Good grief!" groaned the ones who had stars at the first.
"We're *still* the best Sneetches and they are the worst.
But, now, how in the world will we know," they all frowned,
"If which kind is what, or the other way round?"

Then up came McBean with a very sly wink
And he said, "Things are not quite as bad as you think.
So you don't know who's who. That is perfectly true.
But come with me, friends. Do you know what I'll do?
I'll make you, again, the best Sneetches on beaches
And all it will cost you is ten dollars eaches."

"Belly stars are no longer in style," said McBean.
"What you need is a trip through my Star-*Off* Machine.
This wondrous contraption will take *off* your stars
So you won't look like Sneetches who have them on thars."
And that handy machine
Working very precisely
Removed all the stars from their tummies quite nicely

Then, with snoots in the air, they paraded about
And they opened their beaks and they let out a shout,
"We know who is who! Now there isn't a doubt.
The best kind of Sneetches are Sneetches without!"

Then, of course, those with stars all got frightfully mad.
To be wearing a star now was frightfully bad.
Then, of course, old Sylvester McMonkey McBean
Invited *them* into his Star-Off Machine.

Then, of course from THEN on, as you probably guess,
Things really got into a horrible mess.

20

All the rest of that day, on those wild screaming beaches,
The Fix-it-Up Chappie kept fixing up Sneetches.
Off again! On again!
In again! Out again!
Through the machines they raced round and about again,
Changing their stars every minute or two.
They kept paying money. They kept running through
Until neither the Plain nor the Star-Bellies knew
Whether this one was that one... or that one was this one
Or which one was what one... or what one was who.

Then, when every last cent
Of their money was spent,
The Fix-it Up Chappie packed up
And he went.

And he laughed as he drove
In his car up the beach,
"They never will learn.
No. You can't teach a Sneetch!"

But McBean was quite wrong. I'm quite happy to say
That the Sneetches got really quite smart on that day,
The day they decided that Sneetches are Sneetches
And no kind of Sneetch is the best on the beaches.
That day, all the Sneetches forgot about stars
And whether they had one, or not, upon thars.

One day, making tracks
In the prairie of Prax,
Came a North-Going Zax
And a South-Going Zax.

And it happened that both of them came to a place
Where they bumped. There they stood.
Foot to foot. Face to face.

"Look here, now!" the North-Going Zax said. "I say!
You are blocking my path. You are right in my way.
I'm a North-Going Zax and I always go north.
Get out of my way, now, and let me go forth!"

"Who's in whose way?" snapped the South-Going Zax.
"I always go south, making south-going tracks.
So you're in MY way! And I ask you to move
And let me go south in my south-going groove."

Then the North-Going Zax puffed his chest up with pride.
"I never," he said, "take a step to one side.
And I'll prove to you that I won't change my ways
If I have to keep standing here fifty-nine days!"

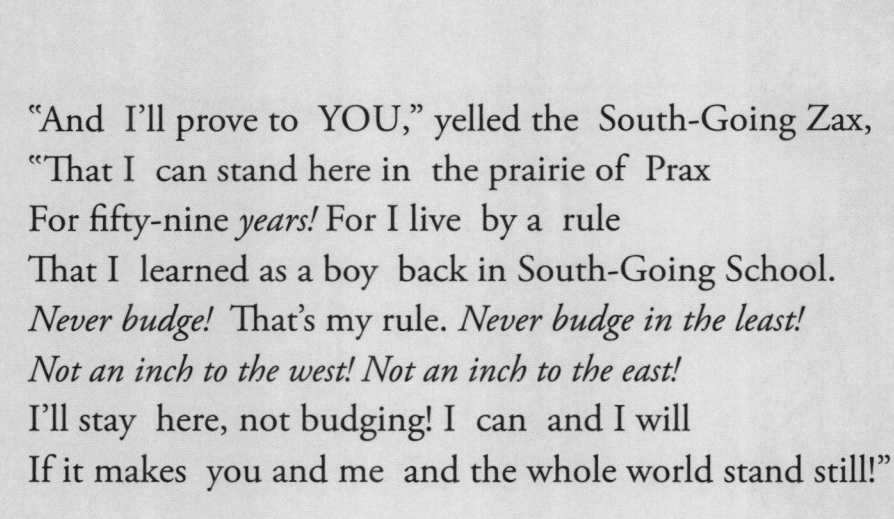

"And I'll prove to YOU," yelled the South-Going Zax,
"That I can stand here in the prairie of Prax
For fifty-nine *years!* For I live by a rule
That I learned as a boy back in South-Going School.
Never budge! That's my rule. *Never budge in the least!*
Not an inch to the west! Not an inch to the east!
I'll stay here, not budging! I can and I will
If it makes you and me and the whole world stand still!"

Well . . .
Of course the world *didn't* stand still. The world grew.
In a couple of years, the new highway came through
And they built it right over those two stubborn Zax
And left them there, standing un-budged in their tracks.

Did I ever tell you that Mrs. McCave
Had twenty-three sons and she named them all Dave?

Well, she did. And that wasn't a smart thing to do.
You see, when she wants one and calls out, "Yoo-Hoo!
Come into the house, Dave!" she doesn't get *one*.
All twenty-three Daves of hers come on the run!

This makes things quite difficult at the McCaves'
As you can imagine, with so many Daves.
And often she wishes that, when they were born,
She had named one of them Bodkin Van Horn
And one of them Hoos-Foos. And one of them Snimm.
And one of them Hot-Shot. And one Sunny Jim.
And one of them Shadrack. And one of them Blinkey.
And one of them Stuffy. And one of them Stinkey.
Another one Putt-Putt. Another one Moon Face.
Another one Marvin O'Gravel Balloon Face.
And one of them Ziggy. And one Soggy Muff.
One Buffalo Bill. And one Biffalo Buff.
And one of them Sneepy. And one Weepy Weed.
And one Paris Garters. And one Harris Tweed.
And one of them Sir Michael Carmichael Zutt
And one of them Oliver Boliver Butt
And one of them Zanzibar Buck-Buck McFate . . .
But she didn't do it. And now it's too late.

W_{ell}...
I was walking in the night
And I saw nothing scary.
For I have never been afraid
Of anything. Not very.

43

Then I was deep within the woods
When, suddenly, I spied them.
I saw a pair of pale green pants
With nobody inside them!

I wasn't scared. But, yet, I stopped.
What *could* those pants be there for?
What *could* a pair of pants at night
Be standing in the air for?

And then they moved! Those empty pants!
They kind of started jumping.
And then my heart, I must admit,
It kind of started thumping.

So I got out. I got out fast
As fast as I could go, sir.
I wasn't scared. But pants like that
I did not care for. No, sir.

After that, a week went by.
Then one dark night in Grin-itch
(I had to do an errand there
And fetch some Grin-itch spinach) . . .
Well, I had fetched the spinach.
I was starting back through town
when those pants raced round a corner
And they almost knocked me down!

I lost my Grin-itch spinach
But I didn't even care.
I ran for home! Believe me,
I had really had a scare!

Now, bicycles were never made
For pale green pants to ride 'em,
Especially spooky pale green pants
With nobody inside 'em!

And the NEXT night, I was fishing
For Doubt-trout on Roover River
When those pants came rowing toward me!
Well, I began to shiver.

And by now I was SO frightened
That, I'll tell you, but I hate to . . .
I screamed and rowed away and lost
My hook and line and bait, too!

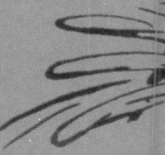

I ran and found a Brickel bush.
I hid myself away.
I got brickels in my britches
But I stayed there anyway.

I stayed all night. The next night, too.
I'd be there still, no doubt,
But I had to do an errand
So, the *next* night, I went out.

I had to do an errand,
Had to pick a peck of Snide
In a dark and gloomy Snide-field
That was almost nine miles wide.

I said, "I do not fear those pants
With nobody inside them."
I said, and said, and said those words.
I said them. But I lied them.

Then I reached inside a Snide bush
And the next thing that I knew,
I felt my hand touch someone!
And I'll bet that you know who.

And there I was! Caught in the Snide!
And in that dreadful place
Those spooky, empty pants and I
Were standing face to face!

I yelled for help. I screamed. I shrieked.
I howled. I yowled. I cried,
"Oh, save me from these pale green pants
With nobody inside!"

But then a strange thing happened.
Why, those pants began to cry!
Those pants began to tremble.
They were just as scared as I!

I never heard such whimpering
And I began to see
That I was just as strange to them
As they were strange to me!

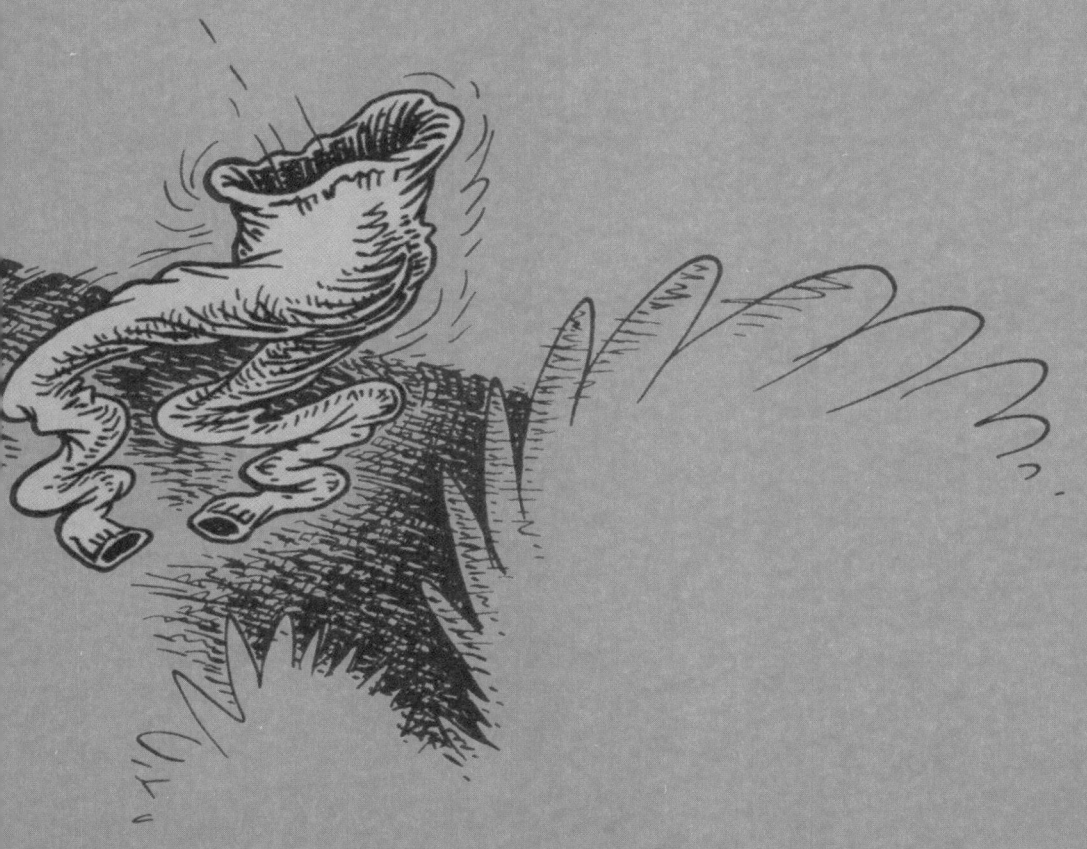

I put my arm around their waist
And sat right down beside them.
I calmed them down.
Poor empty pants
With nobody inside them.

And, now, we meet quite often,
Those empty pants and I,
And we never shake or tremble.
We both smile
And we say
"Hi!"

65

THE CAT IN THE HAT COMES BACK

By

Dr. Seuss

HarperCollins *Children's Books*

The Cat in the Hat
™ & © Dr. Seuss Enterprises, L.P. 1957
All Rights Reserved

A CIP catalogue record for this title is available from
the British Library.
No part of this publication may be reproduced, stored
in a retrieval system or transmitted in any form or by
any means, electronic, mechanical, photocopying,
recording or otherwise, without the prior permission of
HarperCollins Publishers Ltd, 1 London Bridge Street
London SE1 9GF.

3 5 7 9 10 8 6 4

ISBN 978-0-00-820389-4

© 1958, 1986 by Dr. Seuss Enterprises, L.P.
All Rights Reserved
Published by arrangement with
Random House Inc., New York, USA
First published in the UK 1961
This edition published in the UK 2017 by
HarperCollins *Children's Books,*
a division of HarperCollins*Publishers* Ltd
1 London Bridge Street
London SE1 9GF

Visit our website at:
www.harpercollins.co.uk

Printed and bound in India by Replika Press Pvt. Ltd.

This book is produced from independently certified FSC® paper
to ensure responsible forest management.

This was no time for play.
This was no time for fun.
This was no time for games.
There was work to be done.

All that deep,

Deep, deep snow,

All that snow had to go.

When our mother went
Down to the town for the day,
She said, "Somebody has to
Clean all this away.
Somebody, SOMEBODY
Has to, you see."
Then she picked out two Somebodies.
Sally and me.

Well . . .

There we were.

We were working like that

And then who should come up

But the CAT IN THE HAT!

"Oh-oh!" Sally said.

"Don't you talk to that cat.

That cat is a bad one,

That Cat in the Hat.

He plays lots of bad tricks.

Don't you let him come near.

You know what he did

The last time he was here."

"Play tricks?" laughed the cat.
"Oh, my my! No, no, no!
I just want to go in
To get out of the snow.
Keep your mind on your work.
You just stay there, you two.
I will go in the house
And find something to do."

Then that cat went right in!
He was up to no good!
So I ran in after
As fast as I could!

Do you know where I found him?

You know where he was?

He was eating a cake in the tub!

Yes he was!

The hot water was on

And the cold water, too.

And I said to the cat,

"What a bad thing to do!"

"But I like to eat cake

In a tub," laughed the cat.

"You should try it some time,"

Laughed the cat as he sat.

And then I got mad.
This was no time for fun.
I said, "Cat! You get out!
There is work to be done.
I have no time for tricks.
I must go back and dig.
I can't have you in here
Eating cake like a pig!
You get out of this house!
We don't want you about!"
Then I shut off the water
And let it run out.

The water ran out.
And then I SAW THE RING!
A ring in the tub!
And, oh boy! What a thing!
A big long pink cat ring!
It looked like pink ink!
And I said, "Will this ever
Come off? I don't think!"

"Have no fear of that ring,"
Laughed the Cat in the Hat.
"Why, I can take cat rings
Off tubs. Just like that!"

Do you know how he did it?
WITH MOTHER'S WHITE DRESS!
Now the tub was all clean,
But her dress was a mess!

Then Sally looked in.

Sally saw the dress, too!

And Sally and I

Did not know what to do.

We should work in the snow.

But that dress! What a spot!

"It may never come off!"

Sally said. "It may not!"

But the cat laughed, "Ho! Ho!
I can make the spot go.
The way I take spots off a dress
Is just so!"

20

"See here!" laughed the cat.
"It is not hard at all.
The thing that takes spots
Off a dress is a wall!"
Then we saw the cat wipe
The spot off the dress.
Now the dress was all clean.
But the wall! What a mess!

"Oh, wall spots!" he laughed.
"Let me tell you some news.
To take spots off a wall,
All I need is two shoes!"

Whose shoes did he use?
I looked and saw whose!
And I said to the cat,
"This is very bad news.
Now the spot is all over
DAD'S £7 SHOES!"

"But your dad will not
Know about that,"
Said the cat.
"He will never find out,"
Laughed the Cat in the Hat.
"His £7 shoes will have
No spots at all.
I will rub them right off
On this rug in the hall."

"But now we have rug spots!"
I yelled. "What a day!
Rug spots! What next?
Can you take THEM away?"

"Don't ask me," he laughed.
"Why, you know that I can!"
Then he picked up the rug
And away the cat ran.

"I can clean up these rug spots
Before you count three!
No spots are too hard
For a Hat Cat like me!"

He ran into Dad's bedroom
And then the cat said,
"It is good that your dad
Has the right kind of bed."

Then he shook the rug!

CRACK!

Now the bed had the spot!

And all I could say was,

"Now what, Cat?

NOW what?"

But the cat just stood still.
He just looked at the bed.
"This is NOT the right kind of a bed,"
The cat said.
"To take spots off THIS bed
Will be hard," said the cat.
"I can't do it alone,"
Said the Cat in the Hat.

"It is good I have some one
To help me," he said.
"Right here in my hat
On the top of my head!
It is good that I have him
Here with me today.
He helps me a lot.
This is Little Cat A."

And then Little Cat A
Took the hat off HIS head.
"It is good I have some one
To help ME," he said.
"This is Little Cat B.
And I keep him about,
And when I need help
Then I let him come out."

And then B said,

"I think we need Little Cat C.

That spot is too much

For the A cat and me.

But now, have no fear!

We will clean it away!

The three of us! Little Cats B, C and A!"

37

"Come on! Take it away!"
Yelled Little Cat A.

"I will hit that old spot
With this broom! Do you see?
It comes off the old bed!
It goes on the T.V."

And then Little Cat B
Cleaned up the T.V.

He cleaned it with milk,
Put the spot in a pan!
And then C blew it out
Of the house with a fan!

39

"But look where it went!"
I said. "look where it blew!
You blew the mess
Out of the house. That is true.
But now you made Snow Spots!
You can't let THEM stay!"

"Let us think about that now,"
Said C, B and A.

"With some help, we can do it!"
Said Little Cat C.
Then POP! On his head
We saw Little Cat D!
Then, POP! POP! POP!
Little Cats E, F and G!

"We will clean up that snow
If it takes us all day!
If it takes us all night,
We will clean it away!"
Said Little Cats G, F, E, D, C, B, A.

They ran out of the house then
And we ran out, too.
And the Big Cat laughed,
"Now you will see something new!
My cats are all clever.
My cats are good shots.
My cats have good guns.
They will kill all those spots!"

But this did not look
Very clever to me.
Kill snow spots with pop guns?
That just could not be!

"All this does is make MORE spots!"
We yelled at the cat.
"Your cats are no good.
Put them back in your hat.

46

"Take your Little Cats G,
F, E, D, C, B, A.
Put them back in your hat
And you take them away!"

    "Oh, no!" said the cat.
    "All they need is more help.
    Help is all that they need.
    So keep still and don't yelp."

Then Little Cat G
Took the hat off his head.
"I have Little Cat H
Here to help us," he said.

"Little Cats H, I, J,
K, L and M.
But our work is so hard
We must have more than them. .
We need Little Cat N.
We need O. We need P.
We need little Cats Q, R, S, T, ,
U and V."

"Come on! Kill those spots!
Kill the mess!" yelled the cats.
And they jumped at the snow
With long rakes and red bats.
They put it in pails
And they made high pink hills!
Pink snow men! Pink snow balls!
And little pink pills!

Oh, the things that they did!
And they did them so hard,
It was all one big spot now
All over the yard!
But the Big Cat stood there
And he said, "This is good.
This is what they should do
And I knew that they would.

"With a little more help,
All the work will be done.
They need one more cat.
And I know just the one."

"Look close! In my hand
I have Little Cat V.
On his head are Cats W,
X, Y and Z."

"Z is too small to see.

So don't try. You can not.

But Z is the cat

Who will clean up that spot!"

"Now here is the Z
You can't see," said the Cat.
"And I bet you can't guess
What he has in HIS hat!

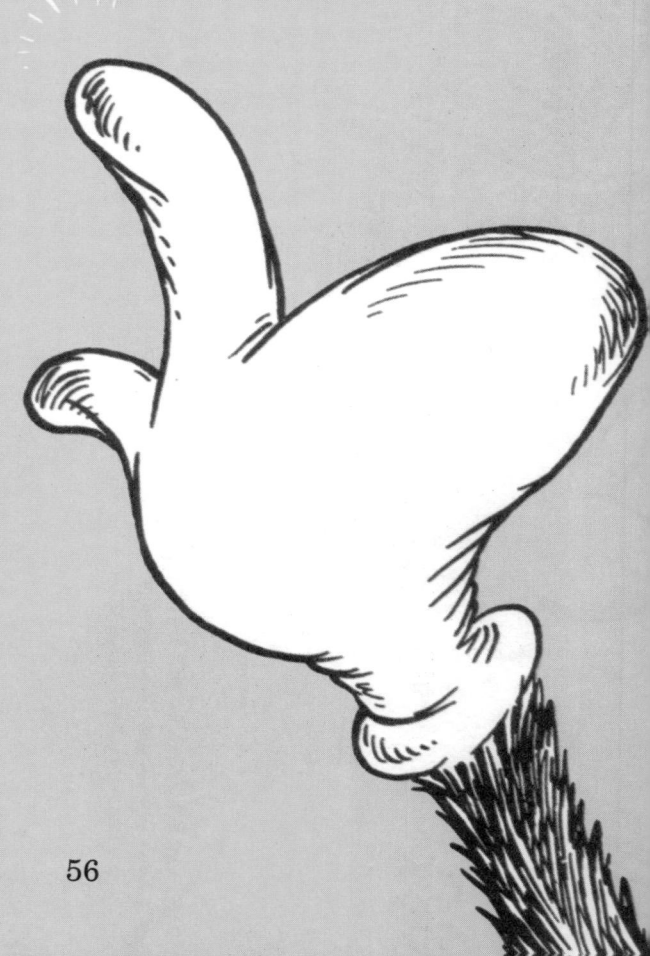

"He has something called VOOM.
Voom is so hard to get,
You never saw anything
Like it, I bet.
Why, Voom cleans up anything
Clean as can be!"
Then he yelled,
"Take your hat off now,
Little Cat Z!
Take the Voom off your head!
Make it clean up the snow!
Hurry! You Little Cat !
One! Two! Three! GO!"

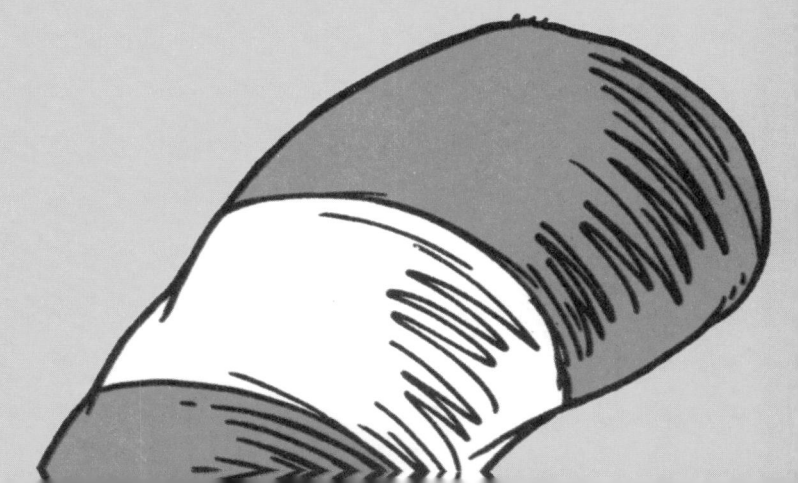

Then the Voom . . .

It went VOOM!

And, oh boy! What a VOOM!

Now, don't ask me what Voom is.

I never will know.

But, boy! Let me tell you

It DOES clean up snow!

"So you see!" laughed the Cat,

"Now your snow is all white!

Now your work is all done!

Now your house is all right!

And you know where my little cats are?"

Said the cat.

"That Voom blew my little cats

Back in my hat.

And so, if you ever

Have spots, now and then,

I will be very happy

To come here again . . .

"... with Little Cats A, B, C, D ...

E, F, G ...

H, I, J, K ...

L, M, N ...

and O,P ..

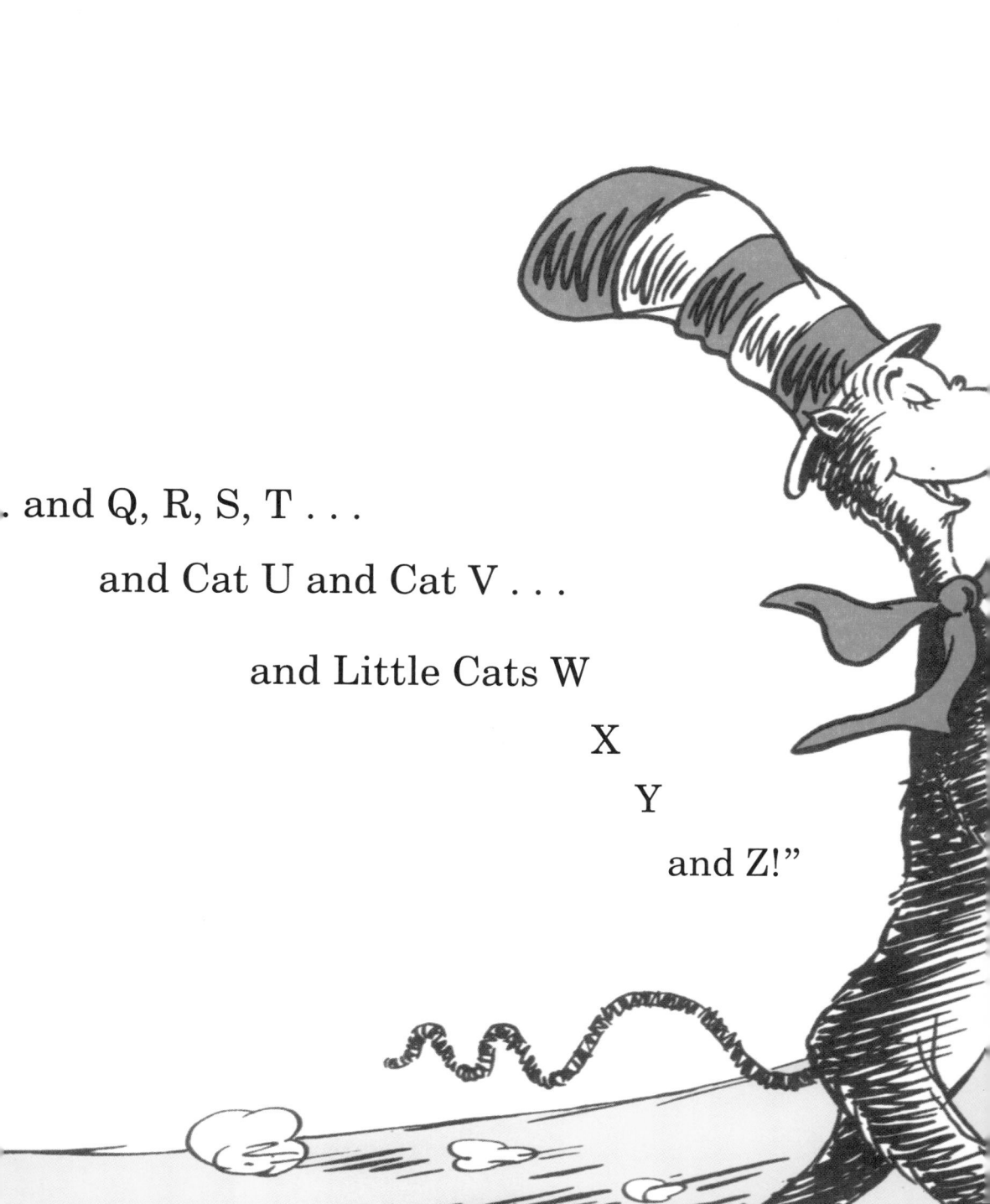

. and Q, R, S, T . . .

and Cat U and Cat V . . .

and Little Cats W

X

Y

and Z!"

SCRAMBLED
EGGS SUPER!

By

Dr. Seuss

HarperCollins *Children's Books*

For LIBBY, ORLO, BRAD AND BARRY CHILDS

™ & © Dr. Seuss Enterprises, L.P.
All Rights Reserved

A CIP catalogue record for this title is available from the
British Library.
No part of this publication may be reproduced, stored
in a retrieval system or transmitted in any form or by
any means, electronic, mechanical, photocopying,
recording or otherwise, without the prior permission of
HarperCollins Publishers Ltd, 1 London Bridge Street
London SE1 9GF

3 5 7 9 10 8 6 4

ISBN 978-0-00-824006-6

Copyright © 1953 by Dr. Seuss Enterprises, L.P.
All Rights Reserved

Published by arrangement with
Random House, Inc., New York USA
First published in the UK 2001
This edition published in the UK 2017 by
HarperCollins *Children's Books*,
a division of HarperCollins*Publishers* Ltd
1 London Bridge Street
London SE1 9GF

www.harpercollins.co.uk

Printed and bound in India by Replika Press Pvt. Ltd.

I don't like to brag and I don't like to boast,
Said Peter T. Hooper, but speaking of toast
And speaking of kitchens and ketchup and cake
And kettles and stoves and the stuff people bake . . .
Well, I don't like to brag, but I'm telling you, Liz,
That speaking of cooks, I'm the best that there is!
Why, only last Tuesday, when mother was out
I really cooked something worth talking about!

You see, I was sitting here, resting my legs
And I happened to pick up a couple of eggs
And I sort of got thinking—it's sort of a shame
That scrambled eggs always taste always the same.

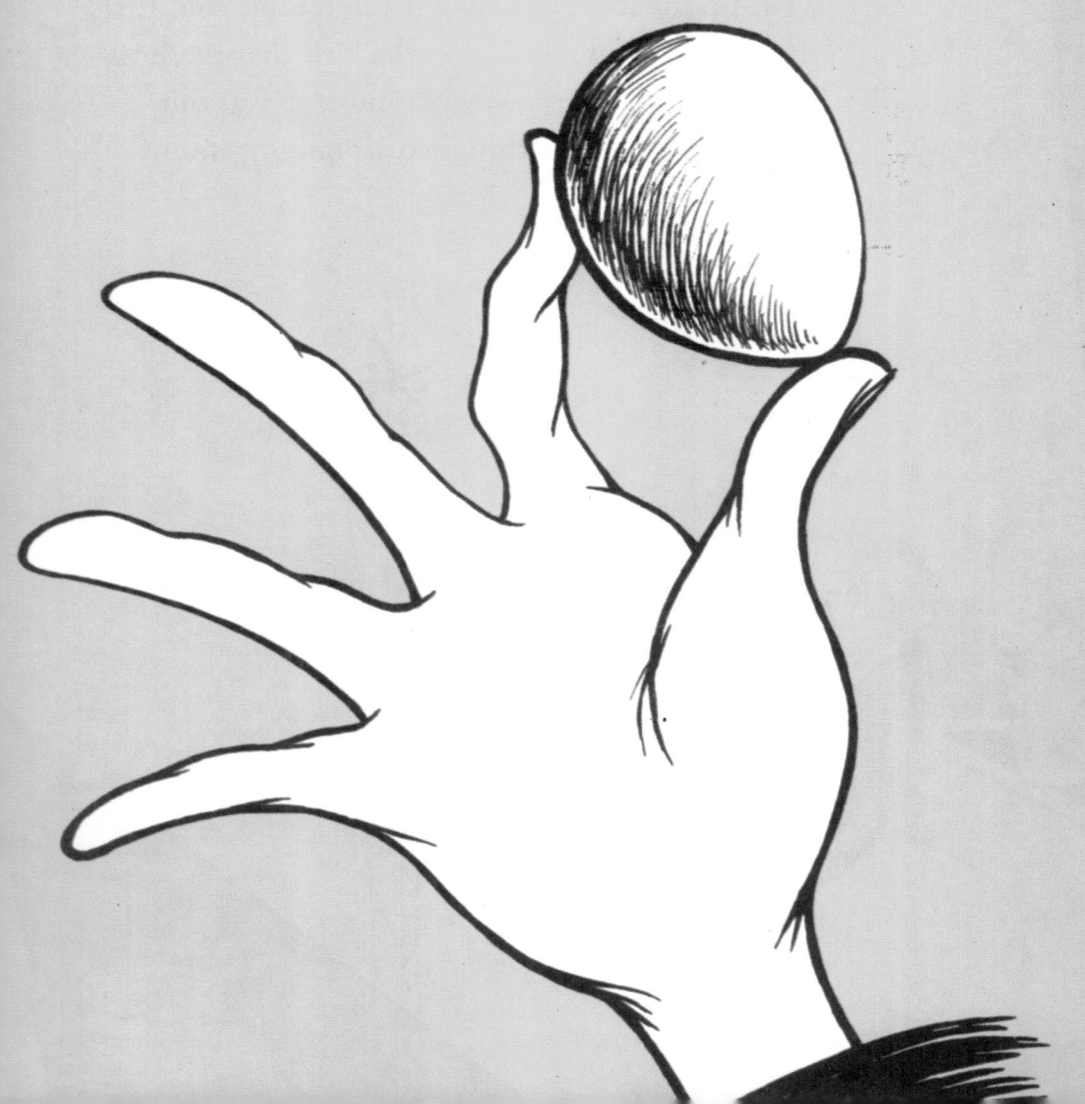

And that's because ever since goodness knows when,
They've always been made from the eggs of a *hen*.
Just a plain common hen! What a dump thing to use
With all of the *other* fine eggs you could choose!

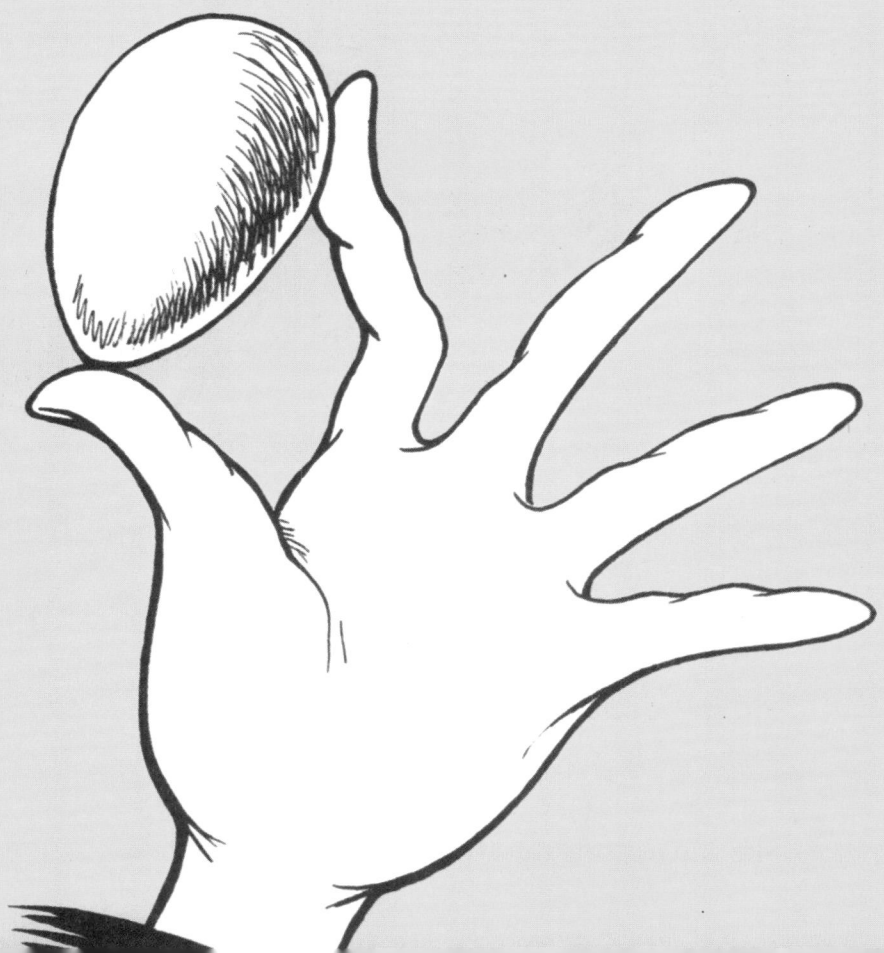

And so I decided that, just for a change,
I'd scramble a *new* kind of egg on the range.
Some fine fancy eggs that no other cook cooks
Like the eggs of the Ruffle-Necked Sala-ma-goox!

A Sala-ma-goox's!
Say! *They* should be good!
So I went out and found some
As quick as I could!

And while I was lugging them back to the house
I happened to notice a Tizzle-Topped Grouse
In a tree down the street. And I knew from her looks
That her egg and the egg of the Sala-ma-goox
Ought to mix mighty well; ought to taste simply super
When scrambled together by Peter T. Hooper.

So I took those eggs home and I frizzled 'em up.
And I added some sugar. Two thirds of a cup.
And a small pinch of pepper. And also a pound
Of horseradish sauce that was sitting around.
And also some nuts.
Then I tasted the stuff
And it tasted quite fine,
But not quite fine enough.

To make the best scramble that's ever been made
A cook has to hook the best eggs ever laid.
So I drove to the country, quite rather far out,
And I studied the birds that were flitting about.
I looked with great care at a Mop-Noodled Finch.
I looked at a Beagle-Beaked-Bald-Headed Grinch.
And, also, I looked at a Shade-Roosting Quail
Who was roosting right under a Lass-a-lack's tail.
And I looked at a Spritz and a Flannel-Wing Jay.
But I just didn't stop. I kept right on my way
'Cause they didn't have eggs. They weren't laying that day.

Then, suddenly . . . *Boy!* Up that hill a short space . . .
Birds! They were laying all over the place!
Great happy gay families with uncles and cousins
All laying fine strictly fresh eggs by the dozens!

Why, I'd have a scramble *more* super than super!
Scrambled eggs Super-dee-Dooper-dee-Booper
Special de luxe à-la-Peter T. Hooper!

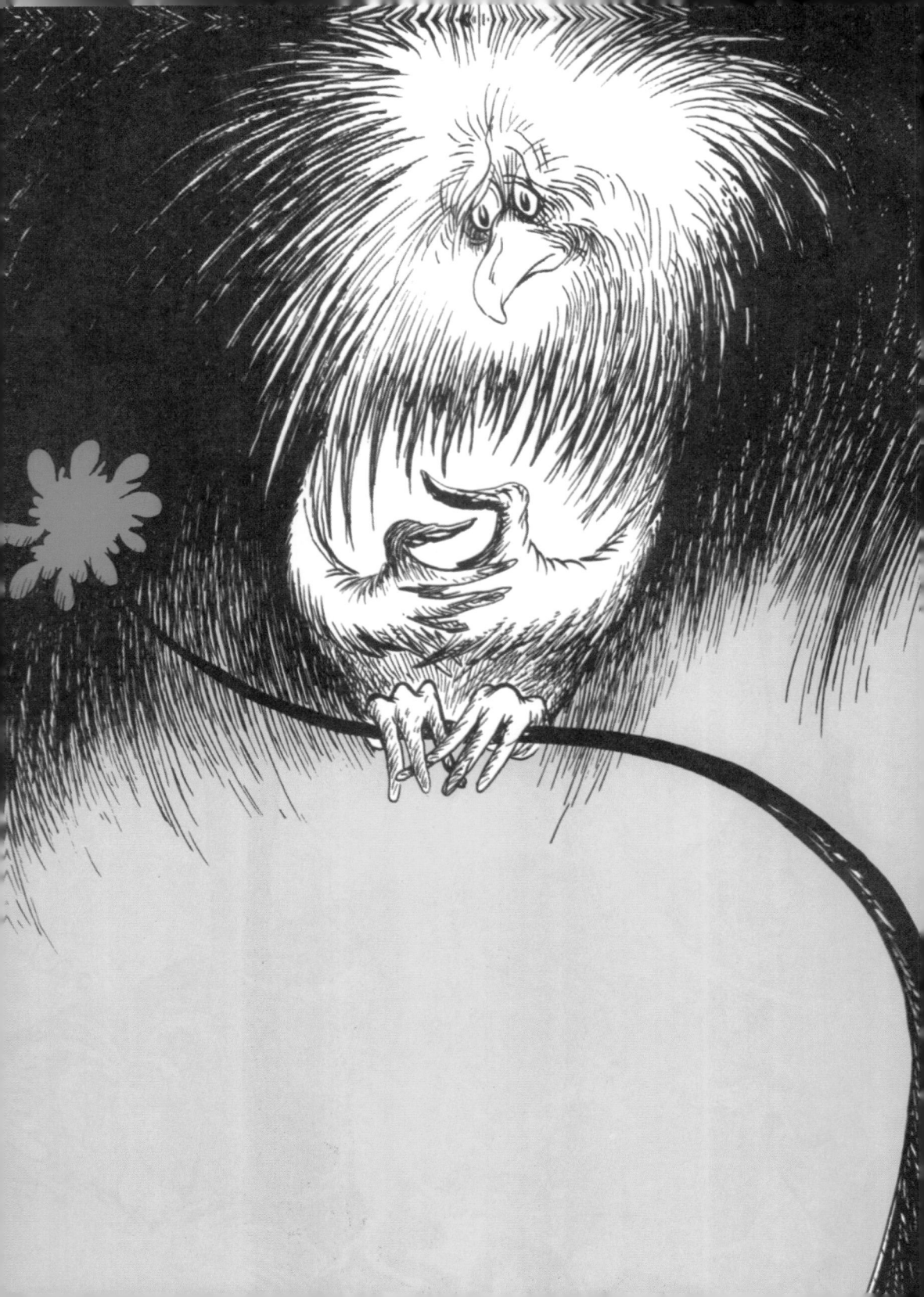

I picked out the eggs in a most careful way.
I only picked those that I knew were Grade-A.
I only took eggs from the very best fowls.
So I didn't take eggs from the Twiddler Owls
'Cause I knew that the eggs of those fellows who twiddle
Taste sort of like dust from inside a bass fiddle.

I went for the kind that were mellow and sweet
And the world's sweetest eggs are the eggs of the Kweet
Which is due to those very sweet trout which they eat
And those trout. . . .well, *they're* sweet 'cause they only eat Wogs
And Wogs, after all, are the world's sweetest frogs
And the reason *they're* sweet is, whenever they lunch
It's always the world's sweetest bees that they munch
And the reason no bees can be sweeter than these . . .
They only eat blossoms off Beezlenut Trees
And these Beezlenut Blossoms are sweeter than sweet
And that's why I nabbed several eggs from the Kweet.

But I passed up the eggs of a bird called a Stroodel
Who's sort of a stork, but with fur like a poodle.
For they say that the eggs of this kind of a stork
Are gooey like glue and they stick to your fork,
And the yolks of these eggs, I am told, taste like fleece
While the whites taste like very old bicycle grease.

The places I hiked to! The roads that I rambled
To find the best eggs that have ever been scrambled!
I hunted new birds along wild tangled trails,
Through gullies and gulches, down dingles and dales.
I wriggled my way and I crawled at a creep
Through a forest of ferns that was forty miles deep.
And I mushed through the brush till I found a fine Kwigger
Whose eggs are as big as a pin head, no bigger.

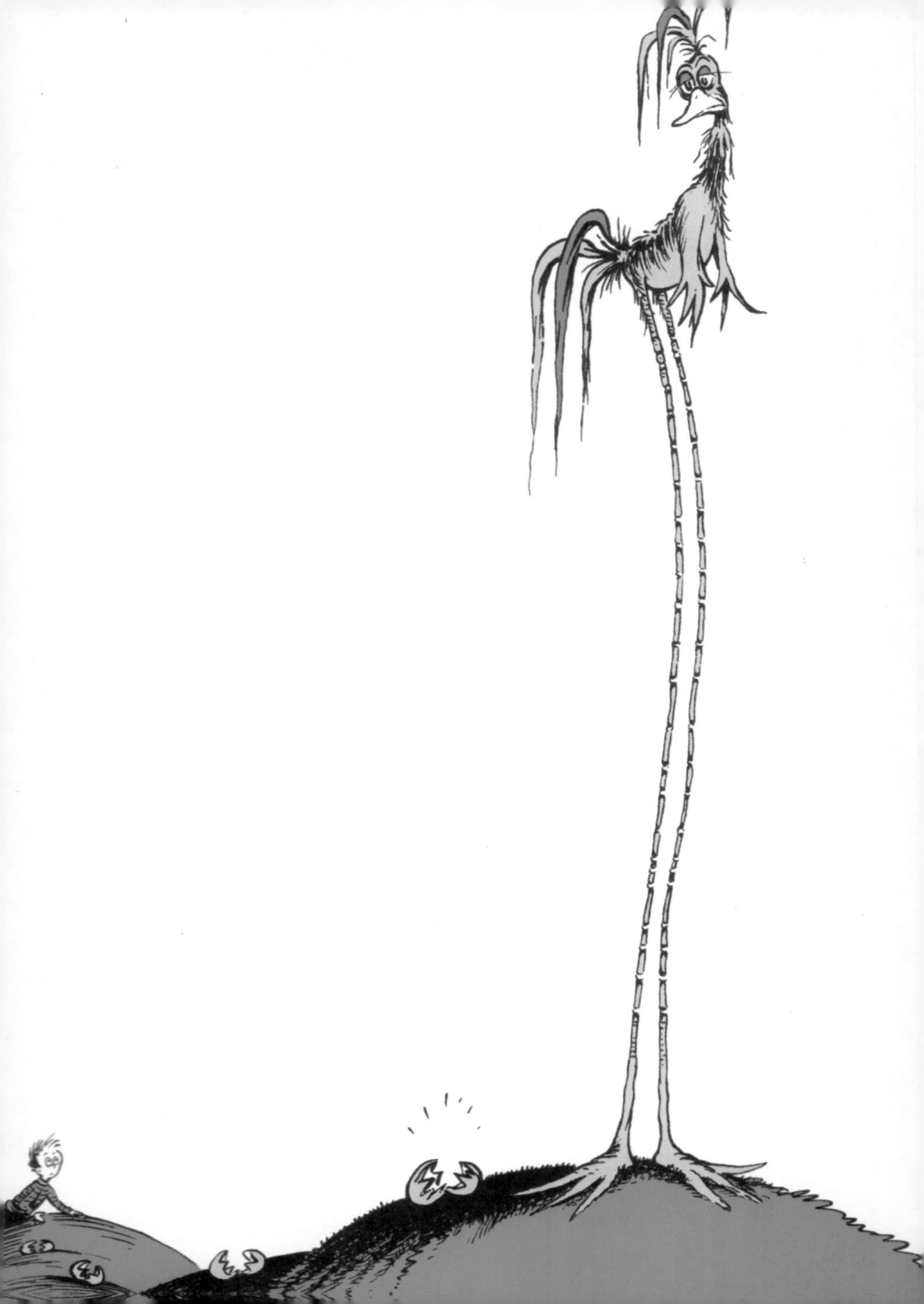

Then I went for the eggs of a Long-Legger Kwong.
Now this Kwong . . . well, she's built just a little bit wrong,
For her legs are so terribly, terribly long
That she has to lay eggs twenty feet in the air
And they drop, with a plop, to the ground from up there!
So unless you can catch 'em before the eggs crash
You haven't got eggs. You've got Long-Legger hash.

Eggs!! I'd collected three hundred and two!
But I needed still more! And I suddenly knew
That the job was too big for one fellow to do.
So I telegraphed north to some friends near Fa-Zoal
Which is ten miles or so just beyond the North Pole.
And they all of them jumped in their Katta-ma-Side,
Which is sort of a boat made of sea-leopard's hide,
Which they sailed out to sea to go looking for Grice,
Which is sort of a bird which lays eggs on the ice,
Which they grabbed with a tool which is known as a Squitsch,
'Cause those eggs are too cold to be touched without which.

And while they were sending those eggs, I got word of
A bird that does something that's almost unheard of!
It's hard to believe, but this bird called the Pelf
Lays eggs that are three times as big as herself!
How that Pelf ever learned such a difficult trick
I never found out. but I found that egg quick.
And I managed to get it down out of the nest
And home to the kitchen along with the rest.

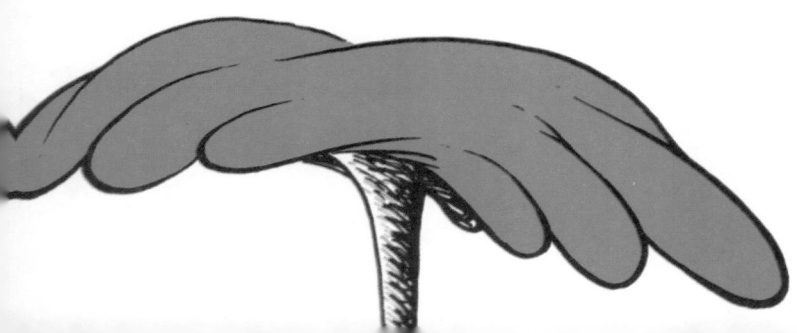

But I didn't stop then, 'cause I knew of some ducks
By the name of the Single-File Zummzian Zuks
Who stroll, single file, through the mountains of Zumms
Quite oddly enough, with their eggs on their thumbs,
And some fellows in Zummz whom I happened to know
Just happened to capture a thousand or so,
And they wrapped up their eggs and they mailed them by air
Marked Special Delivery, Handle with Care.

I needed *more* halpers! And so for assistance
I called up a fellow, named Ali, long distance,
And Ali, as soon as he hung up the phone,
Picked up a small basket and started alone
To climb the steep crags and the jags of Mt. Strookoo
To fetch me the egg of a Mt. Strookoo Cuckoo.
Now these Mt. Strookoo Cuckoos
Are rather small gals . . .

But these Mt. Strookoo Cuckoos have lots of big pals!
They dived from the skies with wild cackling shrieks
And they jabbed at his legs and they stabbed at his cheeks
With their yammering, klammering, hammering beaks,
But Ali, brave Ali, he fought his way through
And he send me that eggs as I knew he would do
For my Scrambled Eggs Super-dee-Dooper-dee-Booper
Special de luxe à-la-Peter T. Hooper!

In the meanwhile, of course, I was keeping real busy
Collecting the eggs of the three-eyelashed Tizzy.
They're quite hard to reach, so I rode on the top
Of a Ham-ikka-Schnim-ikka-Schnam-ikka Schnopp.

Then I found a great flock of South-West-Facing Cranes
And I guess they've got something that's wrong with their brains.
For this kind of a crane, when she's guarding her nest,
Will always stand facing precisely South West.
So to get at those eggs wasn't hard in the least.
I came form behind. From, precisely, North East.

And I captured the eggs of a Grickily Gractus
Who lays 'em up high in a prickily cactus.

Then I went for some Ziffs. They're exactly like Zuffs,
But the Ziffs live on cliffs and the Zuffs live on bluffs.
And, seeing how bluffs are exactly like cliffs,
It's mighty hard telling the Zuffs from the Ziffs.
But I *know* that the egg that I got from the bluffs,
If it wasn't a ziff's from the cliffs, was a Zuff's.

Now I needed the egg of a Moth-Watching Sneth
Who's a bird who's so big she scares people to death!
And this awful big bird . . . Well, the reason they name her
The Moth-Watching Sneth is 'cause that's how they tame her.
She likes watching moths. Sort of quiets her mind.
And while she is watching you sneak up behind
And you yank out her egg. So I got one, of course,
With the help of some friends and a very fast horse.

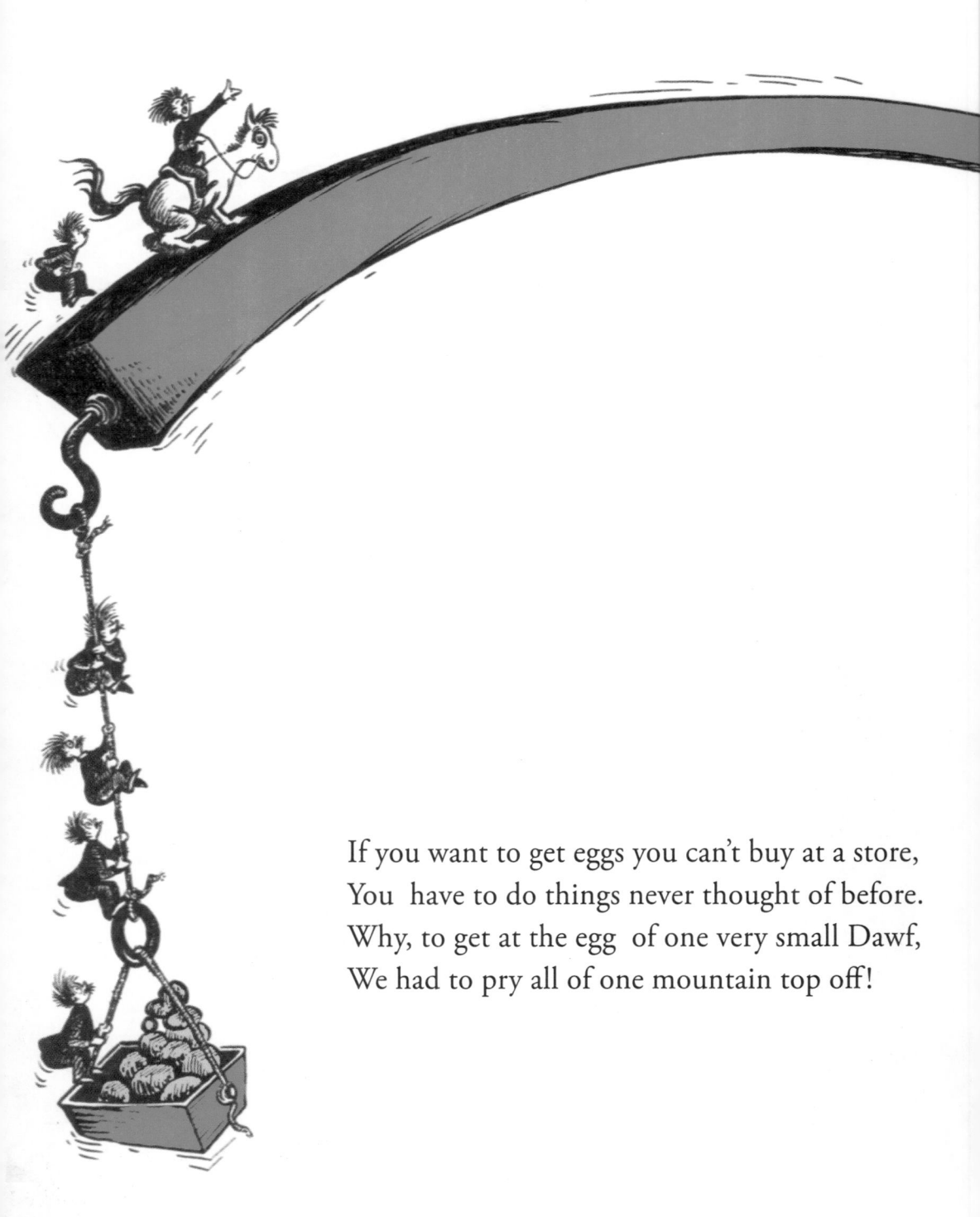

If you want to get eggs you can't buy at a store,
You have to do things never thought of before.
Why, to get at the egg of one very small Dawf,
We had to pry all of one mountain top off!

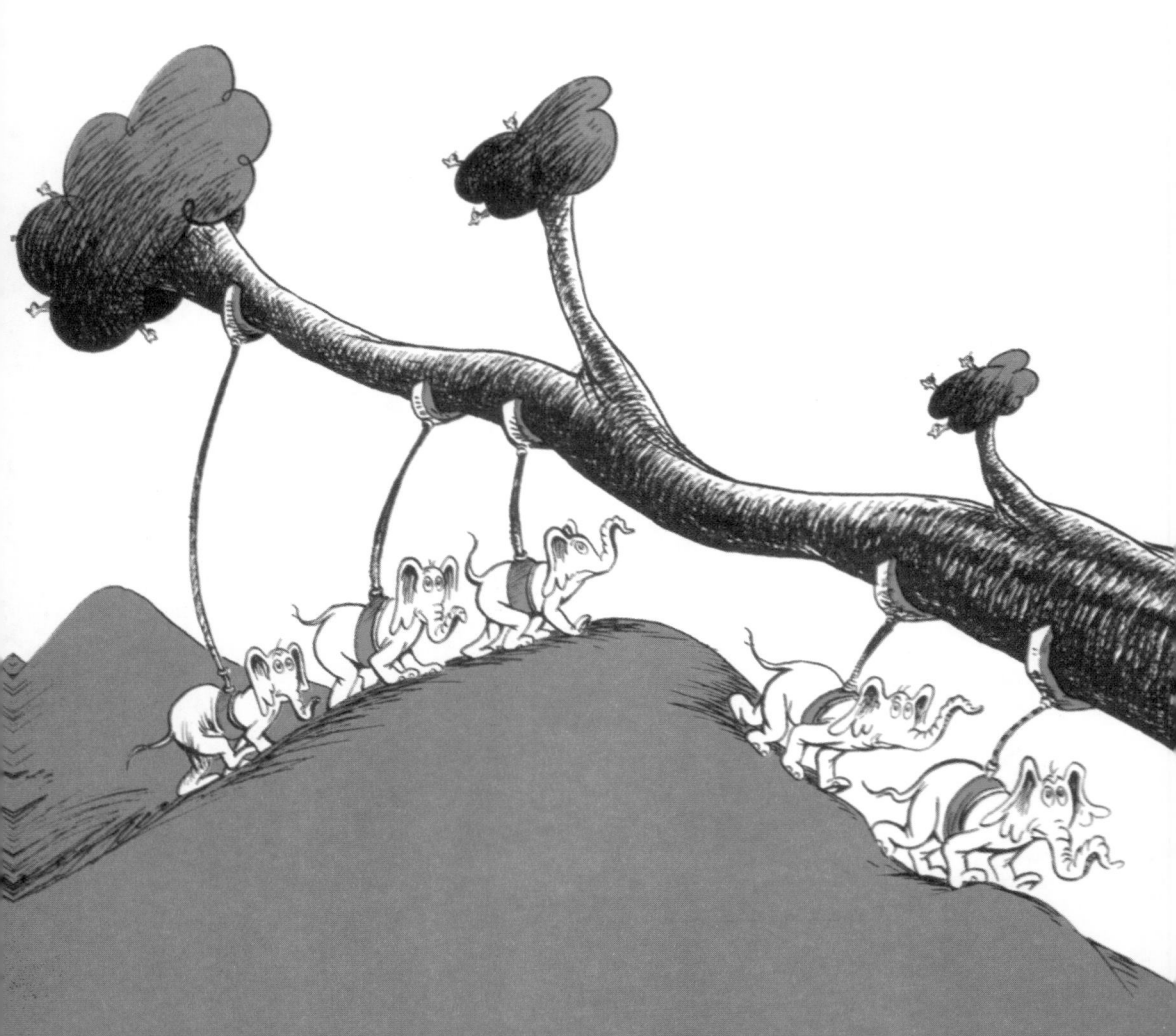

Then I heard of some birds who lay eggs, if you please,
That taste like the air in the holes in Swiss cheese
And they live in big Zinzibar-Zanzibar trees.
So I ordered a tree full. The job was immense,
But I needed those eggs, and said hang the expense!

I still needed one more! And I saved it for last . . .
The egg of the frightful Bombastic Aghast!
And that bird is so mean and that bird is so fast
That I had to escape on a Jill-ikka-Jast
A fleet-footed beast who can run like a deer
But looks sort of different. You steer him by ear.

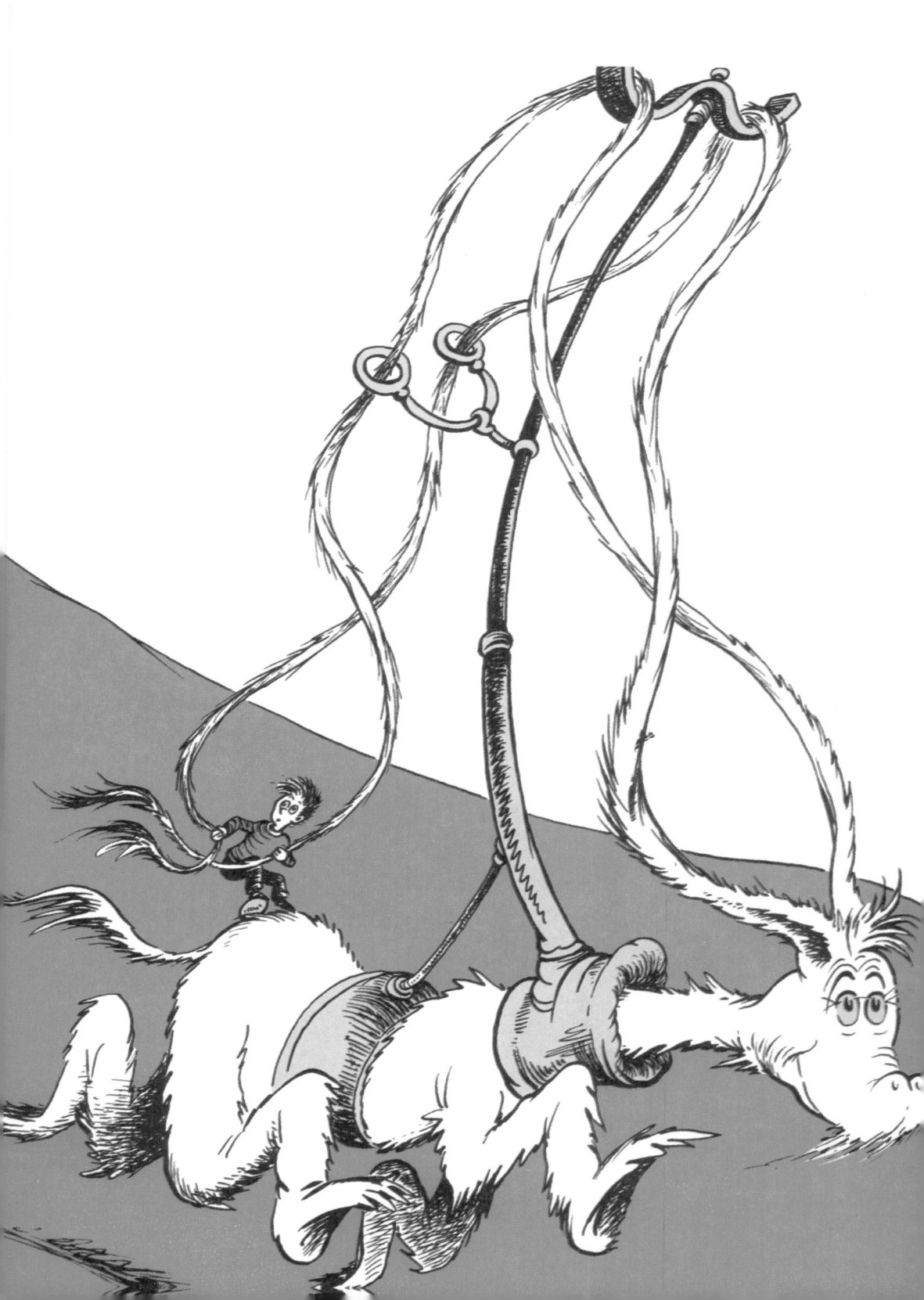

All through with the searching! All through with the looking!
I had all I needed! And now for the cooking.
I rushed to the kitchen, the place where I'd stacked 'em.
I rolled up my sleeves. I unpacked 'em and cracked 'em
And shucked 'em and chucked 'em in ninety-nine pans.
Then I mixed in some beans. I used fifty-five cans.
Then I mixed in some ginger, nine prunes and three figs
And parsley. Quite sparsely. Just twenty-two spring.
Then I added six cinnamon sticks and a clove
And my scramble was ready to go on the stove!

And you know how they tasted?
They tasted just like . . .
Well, they tasted exactly,
Exactly just like . . . like Scrambled eggs Super-
Dee-Dooper-dee-Booper, Special de luxe
à-la-Peter T. Hooper.

YERTLE THE TURTLE AND OTHER STORIES
By
Dr. Seuss

YERTLE THE TURTLE AND OTHER STORIES
By
Dr. Seuss

HarperCollins *Children's Books*

™ & © Dr. Seuss Enterprises, L.P.
All Rights Reserved

A CIP catalogue record for this title is available from the
British Library.
No part of this publication may be reproduced, stored
in a retrieval system or transmitted in any form or by
any means, electronic, mechanical, photocopying,
recording or otherwise, without the prior permission of
HarperCollins Publishers Ltd, 1 London Bridge Street
London SE1 9GF

3 5 7 9 10 8 6 4

ISBN 978-0-00-824003-5

Copyright © 1950, 1951 1958, renewed 1977, 1979, 1986
by Dr. Seuss Enterprises, L.P.

All Rights Reserved
Published by arrangement with Random House Inc.,
New York, USA
First published in the UK in 1963
This edition published in the UK in 2017 by
HarperCollins *Children's Books,*
a division of HarperCollins*Publishers* Ltd
1 London Bridge Street
London SE1 9GF.

www.harpercollins.co.uk

Printed and bound in India by Replika Press Pvt. Ltd.

This Book is for
The Bartletts of Norwich, Vt.
and for
The Sagmasters of Cincinnati, Ohio

YERTLE the TURTLE

On the far away Island of Sala-ma-Sond,
Yertle the Turtle was king of the pond.
A nice little pond. It was clean. It was neat.
The water was warm. There was plenty to eat
The turtles had everything turtles might need.
And they were all happy. Quite happy indeed.

They *were* . . .until Yertle, the king of them all,
Decided the kingdom he ruled was too small.
"I'm ruler," said Yertle, "of all that I see.
But I don't see *enough*. That's the trouble with me.
With this stone for a throne, I look down on my pond
But I cannot look down on the places beyond.
This throne that I sit on is too, too low down.
It ought to be *higher!*" he said with a frown.
"If I could sit high, how much greater I'd be!
What a king! I'd be ruler of all I could see!"

So Yertle, the Turtle King, lifted his hand
And Yertle, the Turtle King, gave a command.
He ordered nine turtles to swim to his stone
And, using these turtles, he built a *new* throne.
He made each turtle stand on another one's back
And he piled them all up in a nine-turtle stack.
And then Yertle climbed up. He sat down on the pile.
What a wonderful view! He could see 'most a mile!

"All mine!" Yertle cried. "Oh, the things I now rule!
I'm king of a cow! And I'm king of a mule!
I'm king of a house! And, what's more, beyond that,
I'm king of a blueberry bush and a cat!
I'm Yertle the Turtle! Oh, marvellous me!
For I am the ruler of all that I see!"

And all through that morning, he sat there up high
Saying over and over, "A great king am I!"
Until round about noon. Then he heard a faint sigh.
"What's *that?*" snapped the king
And he looked down the stack.
And he saw, at the bottom, a turtle named Mack.
Just a part of his throne. And this plain little turtle
Looked up and he said, "Beg your pardon, King Yertle.
"I've pains in my back and my shoulders and knees.
How long must we stand here, Your Majesty, please?"

"SILENCE!" the King of the Turtles barked back.
"I'm king, and you're only a turtle named Mack."

"You stay in your place while I sit here and rule.
I'm king of a cow! And I'm king of a mule!
I'm king of a house! And a bush! And a cat!
But that isn't all. I'll do better than *that*!
My throne shall be *higher*!" his royal voice thundered,
"So pile up more turtles! I want 'bout two hundred!"

"Turtles! More turtles!" he bellowed and brayed.
And the turtles 'way down in the pond were afraid.
They trembled. They shook. But they came. They obeyed.
From all over the pond, they came swimming by dozens.
Whole families of turtles, with uncles and cousins.
And all of them stepped on the head of poor Mack.
One after another, they climbed up the stack.

THEN Yertle the Turtle was perched up so high,
He could see forty miles from his throne in the sky!
"Hooray!" shouted Yertle. "I'm king of the trees!
I'm king of the birds! And I'm king of the bees!
I'm king of the butterflies! King of the air!
Ah, me! What a throne! What a wonderful chair!
I'm Yertle the Turtle! Oh, marvellous me!
For I am the ruler of all that I see!"

Then again, from below, in the great heavy stack,
Came a groan from that plain little turtle named Mack.
"Your Majesty, please . .I don't like to complain,
But down here below, we are feeling great pain.
I know, up on top you are seeing great sights,
But down at the bottom we, too, should have rights.
We turtles can't stand it. Our shells will all crack!
Besides, we need food. We are starving!" groaned Mack.

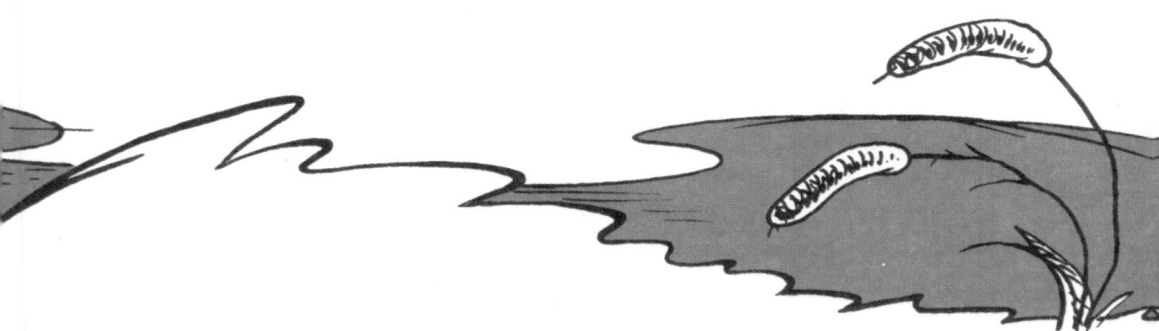

"You hush up your mouth!" howled the mighty King Yertle.
"You've no right to talk to the world's highest turtle.
I rule from the clouds! Over land! Over sea!
There's nothing, no, NOTHING, that's higher than me!"

But, while he was shouting, he saw with surprise
That the moon of the evening was starting to rise
Up over his head in the darkening skies.
"What's THAT?" snorted Yertle. "What IS that thing
That dares to be higher than Yertle the King?
I shall not allow it! I'll go higher still!
I'll build my throne higher! I can and I will!
I'll call some more turtles. I'll stack 'em to heaven!
I need 'bout five thousand, six hundred and seven!"

But, as Yertle, the Turtle King, lifted his hand
And started to order and give the command,
That plain little turtle below in the stack,
That plain little turtle whose name was just Mack,
Decided he'd taken enough. And he had.
And that plain little lad got a little bit mad
And that plain little Mack did a plain little thing.
He burped!
And his burp shook the throne of the king!

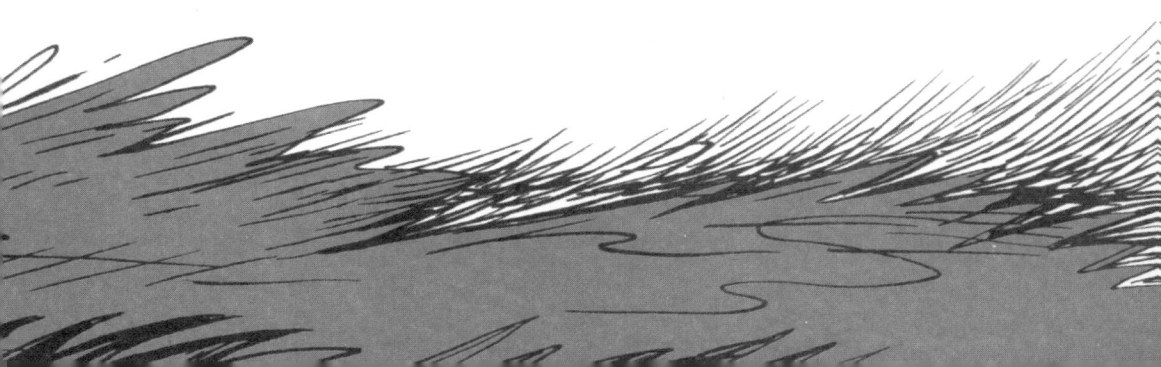

And Yertle the Turtle, the king of the trees,
The king of the air and the birds and the bees,
The king of a house and a cow and a mule . . .
Well, *that* was the end of the Turtle King's rule!
For Yertle, the King of all Sala-ma-Sond,
Fell off his high throne and fell *Plunk*! in the pond!

And today the great Yertle, that Marvellous he,
Is King of the Mud. That is all he can see.
And the turtles, of course. . . all the turtles are free
As turtles and, maybe, all creatures should be.

GERTRUDE McFuzz

There once was a girl-bird named Gertrude McFuzz
And she had the smallest plain tail ever was.
One droopy-droop feather. That's all that she had.
And, oh! That one feather made Gertrude so sad.

For there was another young bird that she knew,
A fancy young birdie named Lolla-Lee-Lou,
And instead of *one* feather behind, she had *two*!
Poor Gertrude! Whenever she happened to spy
Miss Lolla-Lee-Lou flying by in the sky,
She got very jealous. She frowned. And she pouted.
Then, one day she got awfully cross and she shouted:
"This just isn't fair! I have *one*! She has *two*!
I MUST have a tail just like Lolla-Lee-Lou!"

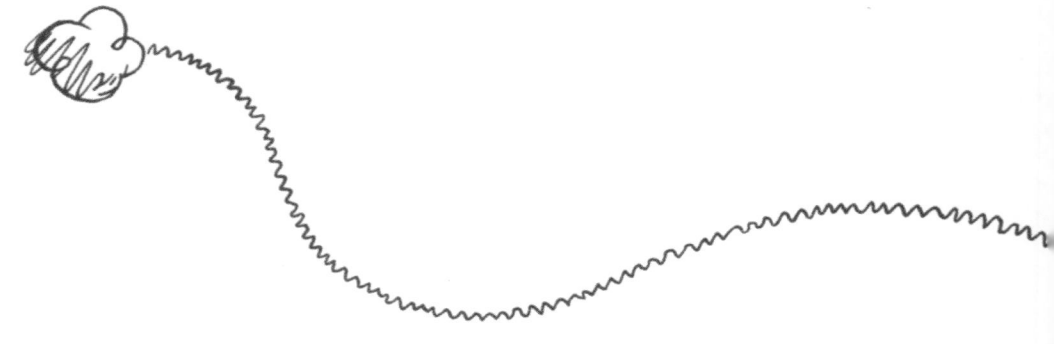

So she flew to her uncle, a doctor named Dake
Whose office was high in a tree by the lake
And she cried, "Uncle Doctor! Oh, please do you know
Of some kind of a pill that will make my tail grow?"
"Tut tut!" said the doctor. "Such talk! How absurd!
Your tail is just right for your kind of a bird."

Then Gertrude had tantrums. She raised such a din
That finally her uncle, the doctor, gave in
And he told her just where she could find such a pill
On a pill-berry vine on the top of the hill.
"Oh, thank you!" chirped Gertrude McFuzz, and she flew
Right straight to the hill where the pill-berry grew.

Yes! There was the vine! And as soon as she saw it
She plucked off a berry. She started to gnaw it.
It tasted just awful. Almost made her sick.
But she wanted that tail, so she swallowed it quick.
Then she felt something happen! She felt a small twitch
As if she'd been tapped, down behind, by a switch.
And Gertrude looked 'round. And she cheered! It was true!
Two feathers! Exactly like Lolla-Lee-Lou!

Then she had an idea! "Now I know what I'll do . . .
I'll grow a tail *better* than Lolla-Lee-Lou!"

"These pills that grow feathers are working just fine!"
So she nibbled *another* one off of the vine!

She felt a *new* twitch. And then Gertrude yelled, "WHEE!
Miss Lolla has only just *two*! I have *three*!
When Lolla-Lee-Lou sees this beautiful stuff,
She'll fall right down flat on her face, sure enough!
I'll show HER who's pretty! I certainly will!
Why, I'll make my tail even prettier still!"

She snatched at those berries that grew on that vine.
She gobbled down four, five, six, seven, eight, nine!
And she didn't stop eating, young Gertrude McFuzz,
Till she'd eaten three dozen! That's all that there was.

Then the feathers popped out! With a *zang*! With a *zing*!
They blossomed like flowers that bloom in the spring.
All fit for a queen! What a sight to behold!
They sparkled like diamonds and gumdrops and gold!
Like silk! Like spaghetti! Like satin! Like lace!
They burst out like rockets all over the place!
They waved in the air and they swished in the breeze!
And some were as long as the branches of trees.
And *still* they kept growing! They popped and they popped
Until, round about sundown when, finally, they stopped.

"And NOW," giggled Gertrude, "The next thing to do
Is to fly right straight home and show Lolla-Lee-Lou!
And when Lolla sees *these*, why her face will get red
And she'll let out a scream and she'll fall right down dead!"

Then she spread out her wings to take off from the ground.
But, with all of those feathers, she weighed ninety pound!
She yanked and she pulled and she let out a squawk,
But that bird couldn't fly! Couldn't run! Couldn't walk!

And all through that night, she was stuck on that hill,
And Gertrude McFuzz might be stuck up there still
If her good Uncle Dake hadn't heard the girl yelp.
He rushed to her rescue and brought along help.

To lift Gertrude up almost broke all their beaks
And to fly her back home, it took almost two weeks.
And *then* it took almost another week more
To pull out those feathers. My! Gertrude was sore!

And, finally, when all of the pulling was done,
Gertrude, behind her, again had just one . . .
That one little feather she had as a starter.
But now that's enough, because now she is smarter.

The BIG BRAG

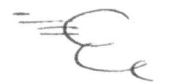

The rabbit felt mighty important that day
On top of the hill in the sun where he lay.
He felt SO important up there on that hill
That he started to brag, as animals will
And he boasted out loud, as he threw out his chest,
"Of all of the beasts in the world, I'm the best!
On land, and on sea . . . even up in the sky
No animal lives who is better than I!"

"What's *that*?" growled a voice that was terribly gruff.
"Now why do you say such ridiculous stuff?"
The rabbit looked down and he saw a big bear.
"*I'm* best of the beasts," said the bear. "And so there!"

"You're not!" snapped the rabbit. "I'm better than you!"
"Pooh!" the bear snorted. "Again I say Pooh!
You talk mighty big, Mr. Rabbit. that's true.
But how can you prove it? **Just what can you DO?"**

"Hmmmm . . ." thought the rabbit,
"Now what CAN I do . . . ?"
He thought and he thought. Then he finally said,
"Mr. Bear, do you see these two ears on my head?
My ears are so keen and so sharp and so fine
No ears in the world can hear further than mine!"

"Humpf!" the bear grunted. He looked at each ear.
"You *say* they are good," said the bear with a sneer,
"But how do *I* know just how far they can hear?"

"I'll prove," said the rabbit, "my ears are the best.
You sit there and watch me. I'll prove it by test."
Then he stiffened his ears till they both stood up high
And pointed straight up at the blue of the sky.
He stretched his ears open as wide as he could.
"*Shhh!* I am listening!" he said as he stood.
He listened so hard that he started to sweat
And the fur on his ears and his forehead got wet.

For seven long minutes he stood Then he stirred
And he said to the bear, "Do you know what I heard?
Do you see that far mountain . . . ? It's ninety miles off.
There's a fly on that mountain. I just heard him cough!
Now the cough of a fly, sir, is quite hard to hear
When he's ninety miles off. But I heard it quite clear.
So you see," bragged the rabbit, "it's perfectly true
That my ears are the best, so I'm better than you!"

The bear, for a moment, just sulked as he sat
For he knew that *his* ears couldn't hear things like *that*.
"This rabbit," he thought, "made a fool out of me.
Now *I've* got to prove that I'm better than he."
So he said to the rabbit, "You hear pretty well.
You can hear ninety miles. *But how far can you smell?*
I'm the greatest of smellers," he bragged. "See my nose?
This nose on my face is the finest that grows.
My nose can smell *any*thing, both far and near.
With my nose I can smell twice as far as you hear!"

"You can't!" snapped the rabbit.
"I can!" growled the bear
And he stuck his big nose 'way up high in the air.
He wiggled that nose and he sniffed and he snuffed.
He waggled that nose and he whiffed and he whuffed.
For more than ten minutes he snaff and he snuff.
Then he said to the rabbit, "I've smelled far enough."

"All right," said the rabbit. "Come on now and tell
Exactly how far is the smell that you smell?"

"Oh, I'm smelling a *very* far smell," said the bear.
"Away past that fly on that mountain out there.
I'm smelling past many great mountains beyond
Six hundred miles more to the edge of a pond."

"And 'way, 'way out there, by the pond you can't see,
Is a very small farm. On the farm is a tree.
On the tree is a branch. On the branch is a nest,
A very small nest where two tiny eggs rest.
Two hummingbird eggs! Only half an inch long!
But my nose." said the bear, "is so wonderfully strong,
My nose is so good that I smelled without fail
That the egg on the left is a little bit stale!
And *that* is a thing that no rabbit can do.
So you see," the bear boasted, "I'm better than you!
My smeller's so keen that it just can't be beat . . ."

"What's that?" called a voice
From 'way down by his feet.
The bear and the rabbit looked down at the sound,
And they saw an old worm crawling out of the ground.

"Now, boys," said the worm, "you've been bragging a lot.
You both think you're great. But *I* think you are not.
You're not half as good as a fellow like me.
You hear and you smell. *But how far can you SEE?*
Now, *I'm* here to prove to you big boasting guys
That your nose and your ears aren't as good as my eyes!?

And the little old worm cocked his head to one side
And he opened his eyes and he opened them wide.
And they looked far away with a strange sort of stare
As if they were burning two holes in the air.
The eyes of that worm almost popped from his head.
He stared half an hour till his eyelids got red.
"That's enough!" growled the bear.
"Tell the rabbit and me
How far did you look and just what did you see?"

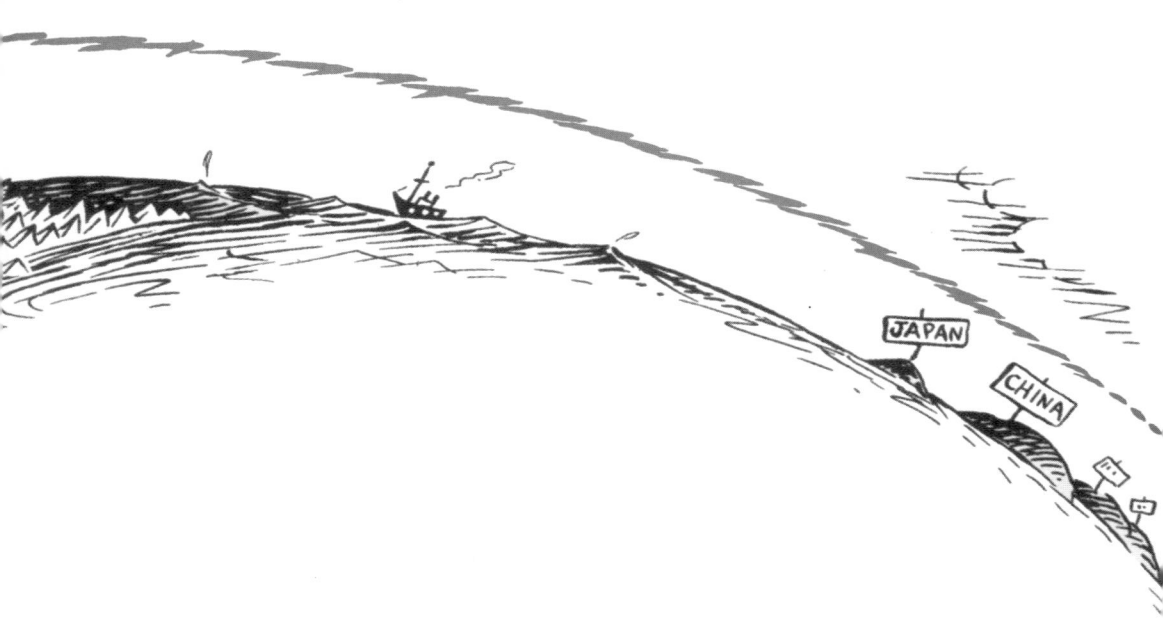

"Well, boys," the worm answered, "that look that I took
Was a look that looked further than *you'll* ever look!
I looked 'cross the ocean, 'way out to Japan.
For I can see further than anyone can.
There's no one on earth who has eyesight that's finer.
I looked past Japan. Then I looked across China.
I looked across Egypt; then took a quick glance
Across the two countries of Holland and France.
Then I looked across England and, also, Brazil.
But I didn't stop there. I looked much farther still.

"And I kept right on looking and looking until
I'd looked round the world and right back to this hill!
And I saw on this hill, since my eyesight's so keen,
The two biggest fools that have ever been seen!
And the fools that I saw were none other than you,
Who seem to have nothing else better to do
Than sit here and argue who's better than who!"

Then the little old worm gave his head a small jerk
And he dived in his hole and went back to his work.

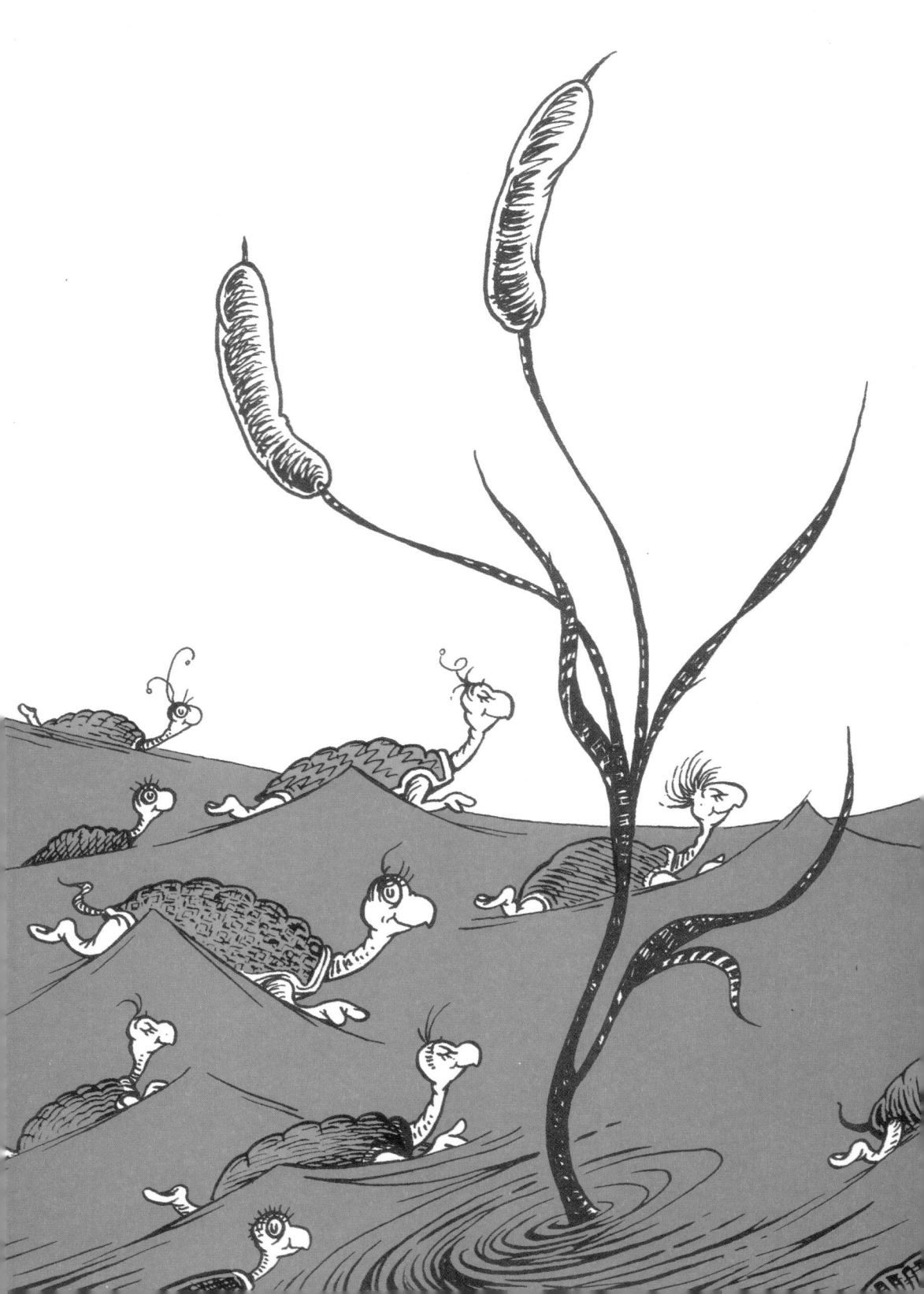

I WISH THAT I HAD DUCK FEET

By

Dr. Seuss

writing as
Theo. LeSieg

Illustrated by B Tobey

HarperCollins *Children's Books*

A CIP catalogue record for this title is available from the
British Library.
No part of this publication may be reproduced, stored
in a retrieval system or transmitted in any form or by
any means, electronic, mechanical, photocopying,
recording or otherwise, without the prior permission of
HarperCollins Publishers Ltd, 1 London Bridge Street
London SE1 9GF

3 5 7 9 10 8 6 4

ISBN 978-0-00-823997-8

Published by arrangement with Random House Inc.,
New York, USA
First published in the UK 1967
This edition published in the UK 2017 by
HarperCollins *Children's Books,*
a division of HarperCollins*Publishers* Ltd
1 London Bridge Street
London SE1 9GF

www.harpercollins.co.uk

Printed and bound in India by Replika Press Pvt. Ltd.

This book is produced from independently certified FSC®paper
to ensure responsible forest management.

I wish
that I had duck feet.
And I can tell you why.
You can splash around in duck feet.
You don't have to keep them dry.

3

I wish that I had duck feet.

No more shoes!

No shoes for me!

The man down at the shoe store

would not have my size, you see.

SHOES

5

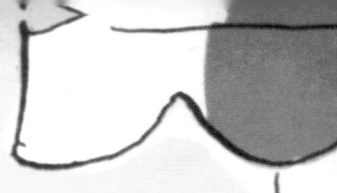

If I had two duck feet,

I could laugh at Big Bill Brown.

I would say, "YOU don't have duck feet!

These are all there are in town!"

6

7

8

I think it would be very good
to have them when I play.
Only kids with duck feet on
can ever play this way.

BUT . . .

My mother would not like them.

She would say, "Get off my floor!"

She would say, "You take your duck feet
and you take them out that door!

"Don't ever come in here again
with duck feet on. Now, DON'T."
SO . . .
I guess I can't have duck feet.
I would like to. But I won't.

11

SO . . .

If I can't have duck feet,

I'll have something else instead . . .

I know what!

I wish I had

two horns up on my head!

13

I wish I had two deer horns.
They would be a lot of fun.
Then I could wear
ten hats up there!
Big Bill can just wear one.

14

15

16

I think they would
be very good
to have when I play ball.
Then nobody could stop me.
No, sir! Nobody at all!

17

My horns could carry
books and stuff
like paper, pens and strings
and apples for my teacher
and a lot of other things!

BUT . . .
If I had
big deer horns,
I would never
get a ride.

I could never use the school bus.
I could never get inside!

21

AND SO . . .

I won't have deer horns.

I'll have something else instead.

I wish I had a whale spout.

A whale spout on my head!

When days get hot

it would be good

to spout my spout in school.

And then Miss Banks
would say, " Thanks! Thanks!
You keep our school so cool."

I could play all day in summer.

I would never feel the heat.

I would beat Big Bill at tennis.

I would play him off his feet.

BUT . . .

My mother would not like it.

I know just what she would say:

"Not in the house!

You turn that off!

You take that spout away."

I know that she would tell me,
"I don't want that spout about!"
And when Mother
does not want a thing,
it's O–U–T. It's out!

29

AND SO . . .

I will not have one.

I don't wish to be a whale.

I think
it would be better
if I had
a long, long tail.

I wish I had a long, long tail.

Some day I will. I hope.

And then I'll show

the kids in town

new ways to jump a rope!

33

If I had a long, long tail
I know what I would like.
I would like to ride down our street
pulling girls behind my bike.

34

I wish I had a long, long tail.
And I can tell you why.
I could hit a fly ten feet away
and hit him in the eye.

I know Miss Banks would like this.
She would smile and she would say,
"No other boy in town can hit
a fly so far away."

BUT . . .

If I had a long, long tail,

I know that Big Bill Brown

would tie me in a tree!

He would!

Then how would I get down?

I don't think that I would like it
with my tail tied in a tree.
The more I think about it . . . NO!
No long, long tail for me.

AND SO . . .

If I can't have a tail,

I'll have a long, long nose!

A nose just like an elephant's,

the longest nose that grows.

I wish I had a long, long nose

and I can tell you why.

I think it would

be very good

to get at things up high.

41

Every kid in town would love it.

Every kid but Big Bill Brown.

And every time I saw him

I would sneeze

and blow him down.

KERCHOO!

43

I could help the firemen!
My nose would be just right.
I could help them put out fires
a hundred times a night.

44

45

Oh, I would do a lot of things
that no one ever did.
And everyone in town would say,
"Just watch that long-nose kid!"

47

BUT . . .

If I had a long, long nose,

I know what Dad would do.

My dad would make me wash the car!

The house and windows, too!

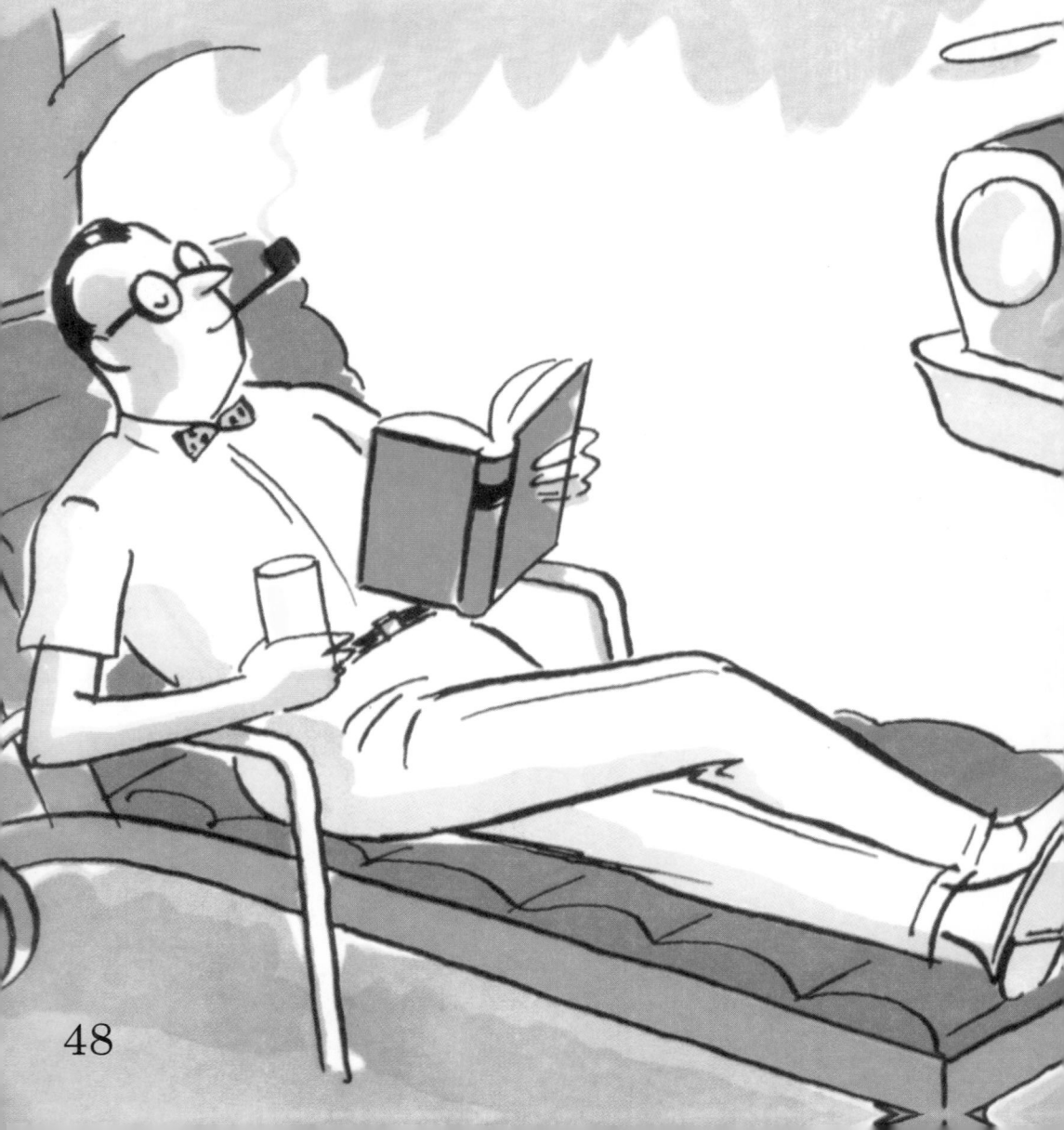

49

50

My dad would make me work all day
and wash things with that hose!
I guess it would not be so good
to have a long, long nose.

51

NOW . . .

Let me think about it.

All these things I want are bad.
And so I wish . . .
I wish . . . I wish . . .
What DO I wish I had? . . .

I know what!

I know just what!

I know just what to do!

I WISH THAT I HAD ALL THOSE

THINGS!

I'd be a Which-What-Who!

If I could be a Which-What-Who,
I'd jump high in the air.
I'd splash and spout
and run about.
I'd give the town a scare!

55

BUT . . .

The people would not like it.

They would be so scared, I bet,

they would call the town policemen.

They would catch me in a net!

56

They would put me in the zoo house
with my horns and nose and feet.
And hay, just hay,
two times a day
is all I'd get to eat.

LION

59

I think I would be very sad
when people came to call.
SO . . .
I don't think
a Which-What-Who
would be much fun at all.

60

61

62

AND SO . . .

I think

there are some things

I do not wish to be.

And that is why

I think that I

just wish to be like ME.

63

HOP ON POP

By
Dr. Seuss

HarperCollins *Children's Books*

HarperCollins
PUBLISHERS
Since 1817

The Cat in the Hat
™ & © Dr. Seuss Enterprises, L.P. 1957
All Rights Reserved

A CIP catalogue record for this title is available from
the British Library.
No part of this publication may be reproduced, stored
in a retrieval system or transmitted in any form or by
any means, electronic, mechanical, photocopying,
recording or otherwise, without the prior permission of
HarperCollins Publishers Ltd, 1 London Bridge Street
London SE1 9GF.

3 5 7 9 10 8 6 4

ISBN 978-0-00-820390-0

© 1963, 1991 by Dr. Seuss Enterprises, L.P.
All Rights Reserved
Published by arrangement with
Random House Inc., New York, USA
First published in the UK 1964
This edition published in the UK 2017 by
HarperCollins *Children's Books,*
a division of HarperCollins*Publishers* Ltd
1 London Bridge Street
London SE1 9GF

Visit our website at:
www.harpercollins.co.uk

Printed and bound in India by Replika Press Pvt. Ltd.

MIX
Paper from
responsible sources
FSC® C016779

This book is produced from independently certified FSC® paper
to ensure responsible forest management.

UP
PUP

Pup is up.

CUP
PUP

Pup in cup

PUP
CUP

Cup on pup

MOUSE HOUSE

Mouse on house

HOUSE
MOUSE

House on mouse

ALL
TALL

We all are tall.

ALL
SMALL

We all are small.

ALL
BALL

We all play ball

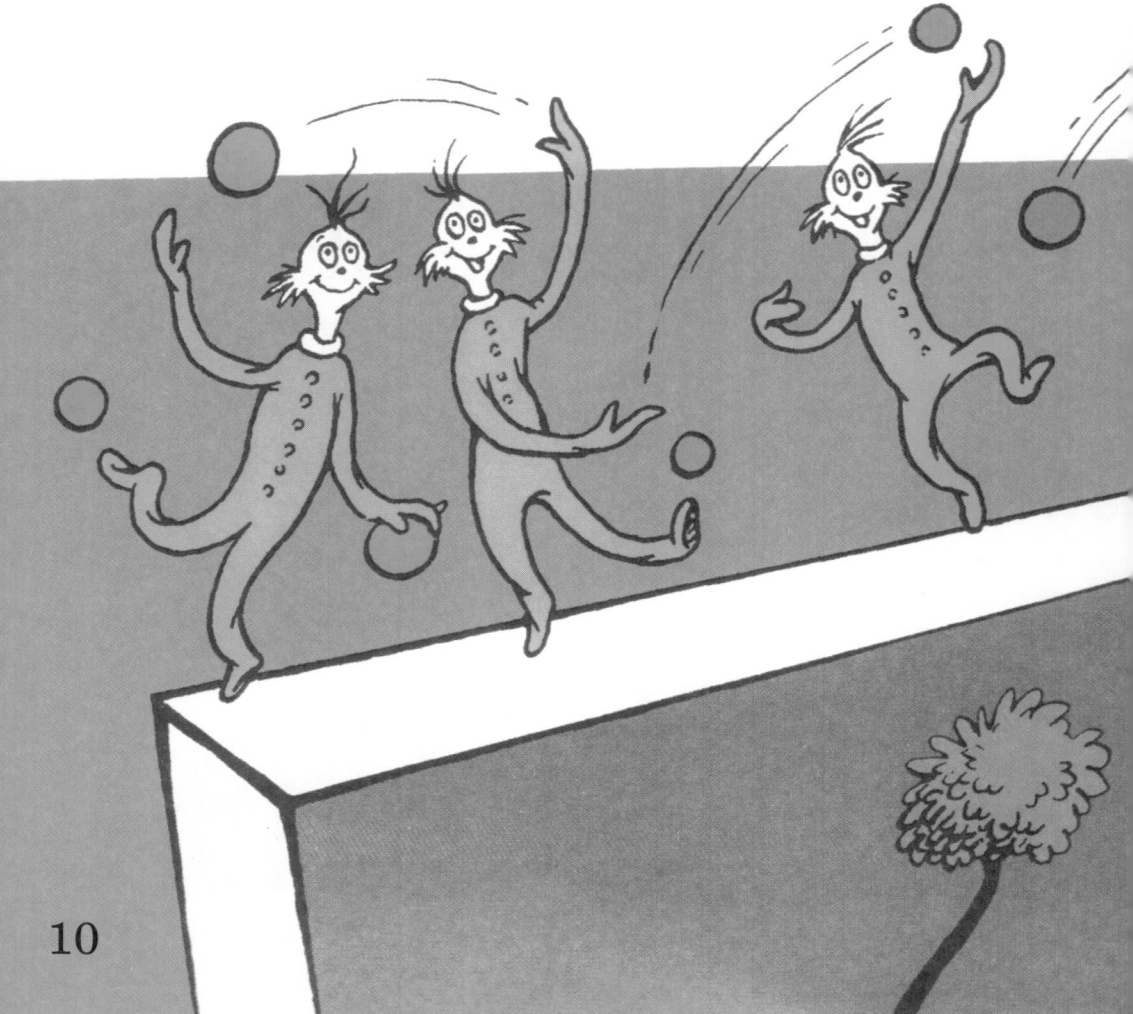

BALL
WALL

up on a wall.

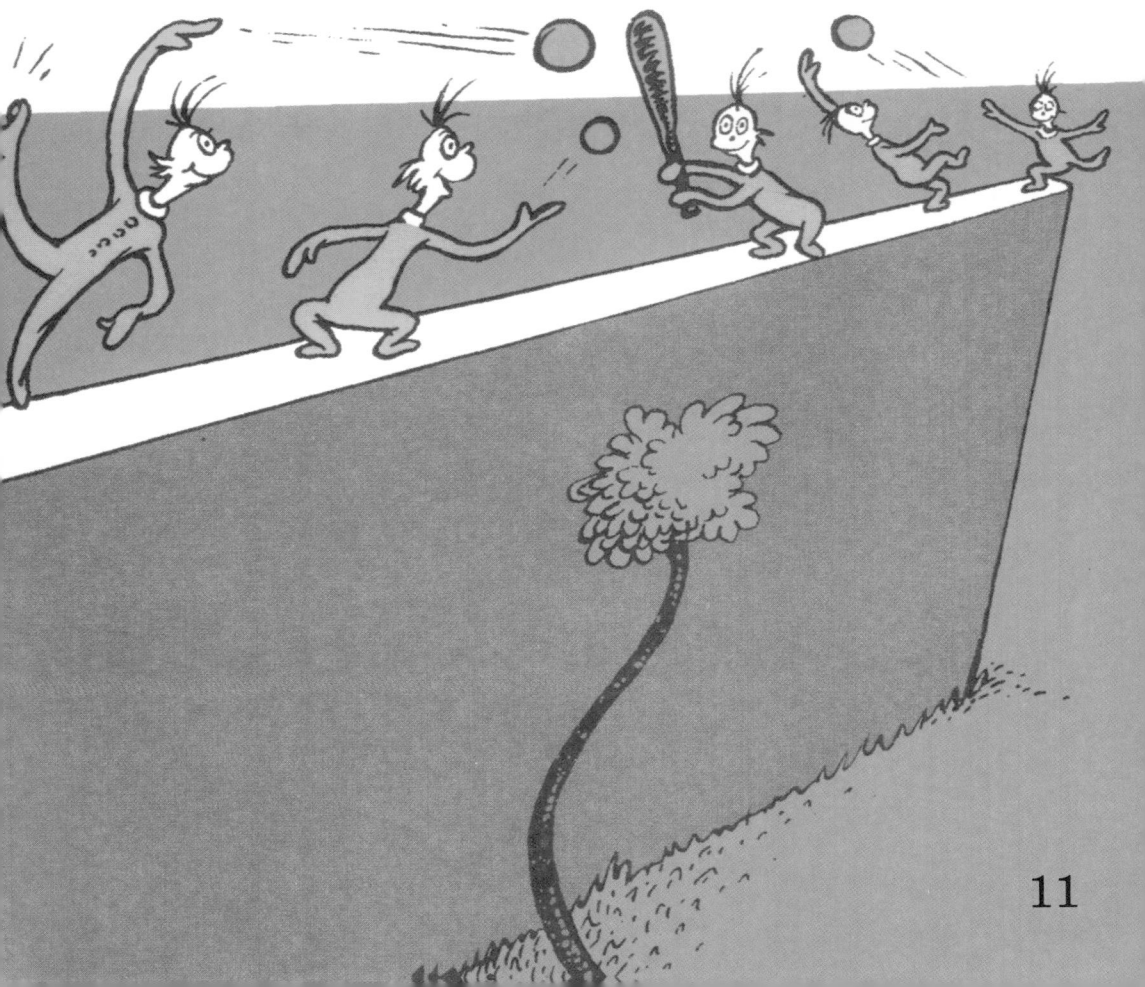

ALL
FALL

Fall off the wall

DAY
PLAY

We play all day.

NIGHT
FIGHT

We fight all night.

HE
ME

He is after me.

HIM
JIM

Jim is after him.

SEE
BEE

We see a bee.

SEE
BEE
THREE

Now we
see three.

THREE
TREE

Three fish in a tree

Fish in a tree?
How can that be?

RED
RED

They call me Red.

RED
BED

I am in bed.

RED
NED
TED
and
ED
in
BED

24

PAT
PAT

They call him Pat.

PAT
SAT

Pat sat on hat.

PAT
CAT

Pat sat on cat.

PAT
BAT

Pat sat on bat.

NO
PAT
NO

Don't sit on that.

31

SAD
DAD
BAD
HAD

Dad is sad
very, very sad.
He had a bad day.
What a day Dad had!

THING
THING

What is that thing?

THING
SING

That thing can sing!

SONG LONG

A long, long song

Good-by, Thing.
You sing too long.

WALK
WALK

We like to walk.

WALK
TALK

We like to talk.

HOP
POP

We like to hop.
We like to hop
on top of Pop.

STOP

You must not
hop on Pop.

Mr. BROWN
Mrs. BROWN

Mr. Brown upside down

Pup up

Brown down

44

Pup is down.
Where is Brown?

45

WHERE IS BROWN?
THERE IS BROWN!

Mr. Brown is out of town.

BACK
BLACK

Brown came back.

Brown came back
with Mr. Black.

SNACK SNACK

Eat a snack.

Eat a snack
with Brown and Black.

JUMP
BUMP

He jumped.
He bumped.

FAST
PAST

He went past fast.

WENT
TENT
SENT

He went into the tent.

I sent him out of the tent.

WET
GET

Two dogs get wet.

HELP
YELP

They yelp for help.

HILL
WILL

Will went up the hill.

WILL
HILL
STILL

Will is
up the hill still.

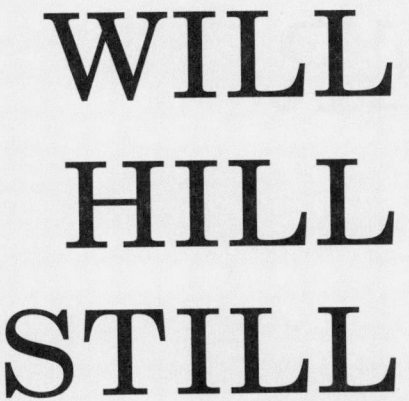

FATHER
MOTHER

SISTER
BROTHER

58

That one is
my other brother.

My brothers read
a little bit.

Little
words
like

My father
can read
big words, too

like...............

CONSTANTINOPLE

and

TIMBUKTU

SAY
SAY

What does this say?

seehemewe
patpuppop
hethreetreebee
tophopstop

Ask me tomorrow
but not today.

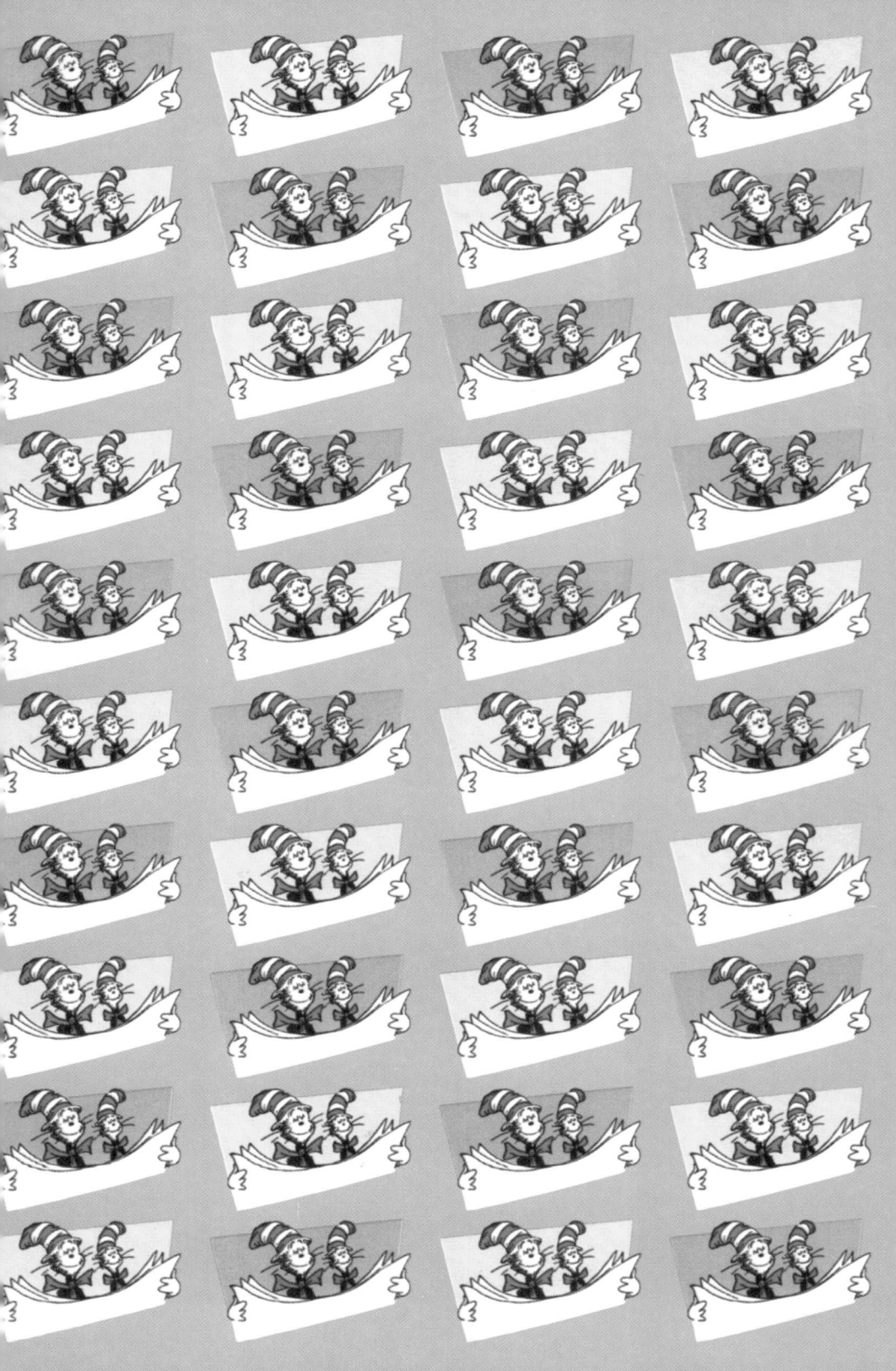

I CAN READ WITH MY EYES SHUT!

By

Dr. Seuss

I CAN READ WITH MY EYES SHUT!

By

Dr. Seuss

HarperCollins *Children's Books*

™ & © Dr. Seuss Enterprises, L.P.
All Rights Reserved

A CIP catalogue record for this title is available from the
British Library.
No part of this publication may be reproduced, stored
in a retrieval system or transmitted in any form or by
any means, electronic, mechanical, photocopying,
recording or otherwise, without the prior permission of
HarperCollins Publishers Ltd, 1 London Bridge Street
London SE1 9GF

3 5 7 9 10 8 6 4

ISBN 978-0-00-824001-1

© 1978 by Dr. Seuss Enterprises, L.P.
All Rights Reserved
A Beginning Beginners, published by arrangement with
Random House Inc., New York, USA
First published in the UK 1979
This edition published in the UK 2017 by
HarperCollins *Children's* Books,
a division of HarperCollins*Publishers* Ltd
1 London Bridge Street
London SE1 9GF

www.harpercollins.co.uk

Printed and bound in India by Replika Press Pvt. Ltd.

For

David Worthen, E.G.*

*(Eye Guy)

I can read
in red.

I can read
in blue.

I can read in
pickle colour
too.

I can read in bed.

And in purple.
And in brown.

I can read
with
my
left eye.

I
can
read
with
my right.

I can read
Mississippi
with my eyes shut tight!

Mississippi

Mississippi,

Indianapolis

and

Hallelujah,

too!

I can read them
with my eyes shut!

That is
VERY HARD
to do!

But it's bad for my hat
and makes my eyebrows
get red hot.
so . . .

reading with my eyes shut
I don't do an awful lot.

And when I keep them open
I can read with much more speed.
You have to be a speedy reader
'cause there's so, so much to read!

You can read about trees . . .

and bees . . .

and knees.

And knees on trees!

And
bees
on
threes!

You can read about anchors.

And all about ants.

You can read about ankles.

And crocodile pants!

You can read about hoses . . .

and how
to smell roses . . .

and what
you should do
about owls on noses!

Young cat! If you keep
your eyes open enough,
oh, the stuff you will learn!
The most wonderful stuff!

You'll learn about . . .

fishbones . . .   and wishbones.

You'll learn
about trombones,
too.

You'll learn
about Jake
the Pillow Snake

and all about
Foo-Foo the Snoo.

You can learn about ice.
You can learn about mice.

Mice on ice.

And
ice
on
mice.

You can learn about
the price of ice.

Nice ice
for sale.
Ten cents a pail.

You can learn about SAD . . .

and GLAD . . .

and MAD!

There are
so many things
you can learn about.
BUT . . . you'll miss
the best things
if you keep
your eyes shut.

The more that you read,
the more things you will know.
The more that you learn,
the more places you'll go.

You might learn
a way to earn
a few dollars.

Or how to make doughnuts . . .

or kangaroo collars.

You can learn to read music
and play a Hut-Zut
if you keep your eyes open.
But <u>not</u> with them shut.

If you read with your eyes shut
you're likely to find
that the place where you're going
is far, far behind.

ELCOME
to
ES-BARRE
DALLAS
SAN DIEGO
LAKE FOREST
SCHENECTADY
ETOUR
Bikes Only
NO EXIT
NO RIGHT TURN
LEFT
?
STOP
REST
ROOMS
8 Miles
SALINA
Kansas
Birthplace
of
Curtis A. Abel
2376 Miles →

SO . . .
that's why I tell you
to keep your eyes wide.
Keep them wide open . . .
at least on one side.

Dr. Seuss's SLEEP BOOK

By

Dr. Seuss

HarperCollins *Children's Books*

For Marie and Bert Hupp

™ & © Dr. Seuss Enterprises, L.P.
All Rights Reserved

A CIP catalogue record for this title is available from the
British Library.
No part of this publication may be reproduced, stored
in a retrieval system or transmitted in any form or by
any means, electronic, mechanical, photocopying,
recording or otherwise, without the prior permission of
HarperCollins Publishers Ltd, 1 London Bridge Street
London SE1 9GF

3 5 7 9 10 8 6 4

ISBN 978-0-00-824005-9

Published by arrangement with Random House Inc.,
New York, USA
First published in the UK 1964
This edition published in the UK 2017 by
HarperCollins *Children's Books*,
a division of HarperCollins*Publishers* Ltd
1 London Bridge Street
London SE1 9GF

www.harpercollins.co.uk

Printed and bound in India by Replika Press Pvt. Ltd.

The news

Just came in
From the County of Keck
That a very small bug
By the name of Van Vleck
Is yawning so wide
You can look down his neck.

This may not seem
Very important, I know.
But it *is*. So I'm bothering
Telling you so.

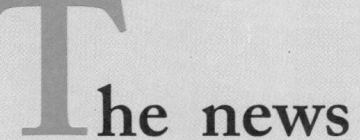

A yawn is quite catching, you see. Like a cough.
It just takes one yawn to start other yawns off.
NOW the news has come in that some friends of Van Vleck's
Are yawning so wide you can look down *their* necks.

At this moment, right now,
Under seven more noses,
Great yawns are in blossom.
They're blooming like roses.

The yawn of that one little bug is still spreading!
According to latest reports, it is heading
Across the wide fields, through the sleepy night air,
Across the whole country toward every-which-where.
And people are gradually starting to say,
"I feel rather drowsy. I've had quite a day."

Creatures are starting to think about rest.
Two Biffer-Baum Birds are now building their nest.
They do it each night,. And quite often I wonder
How they do this big job without making a blunder.
But that is *their* problem.
Not yours. And not mine.
The point is: They're going to bed.
And that's fine.

Sleep thoughts
Are spreading
Throughout the whole land.
The time for night-brushing of teeth is at hand.
Up at Herk-Heimer Falls, where the great river rushes
And crashes down crags in great gargling gushes,
The Herk-Heimer Sisters are using their brushes.
Those falls are just grand for tooth-brushing beneath
If you happen to be up that way with your teeth.

The news just came in from the Castle of Krupp
That the lights are all out and the drawbridge is up.
And the old drawbridge draw-er just said with a yawn,
"My drawbridge is drawn and it's going to stay drawn
'Til the milkman delivers the milk, about dawn.
I'm going to bed now. So nobody better
Come round with a special delivery letter."

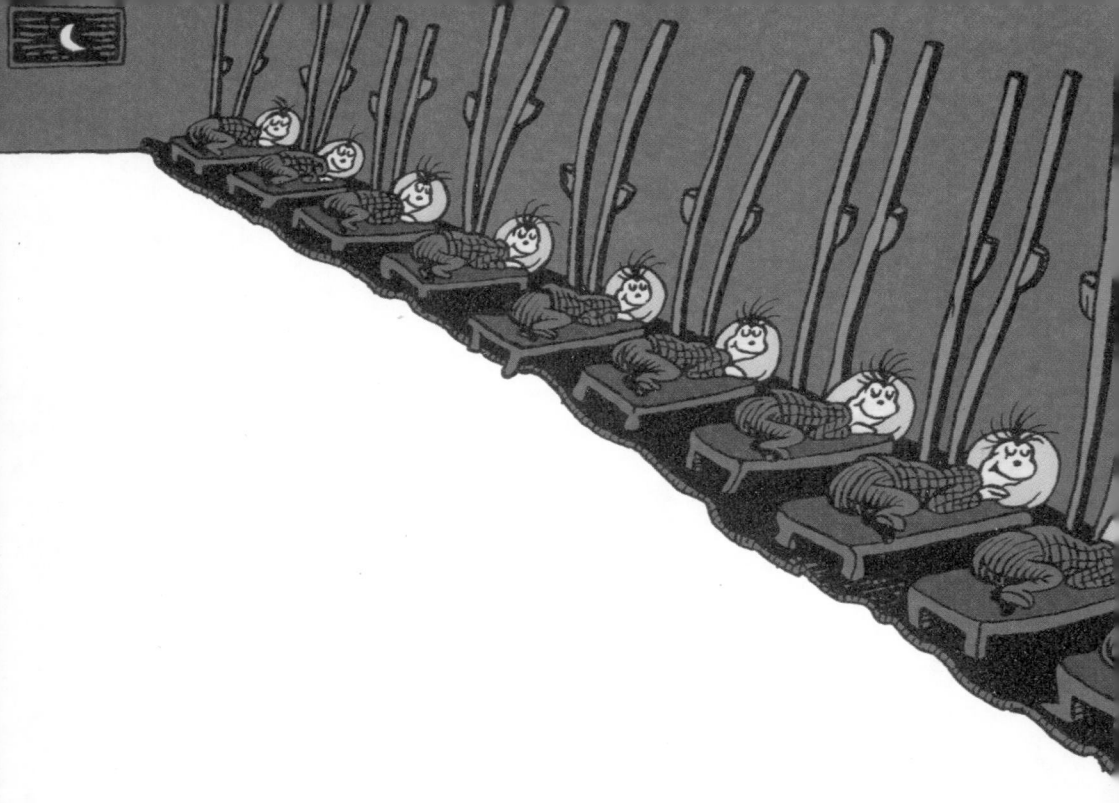

The number
Of sleepers
Is steadily growing.
Bed is where
More and more people are going.
In Culpepper Springs, in the Stilt-Walkers' Hall,
The stilt-walkers' stilts are all stacked on the wall.
The stilt-walker walkers have called it a day.
They're all tuckered out and they're snoozing away.
This is very big news. It's important to know.
And that's why I'm bothering telling you so.

Way out in the west, in the town of Mercedd,
The Hinkle-Horn Honking Club just went to bed.
Every horn has been quietly hung on a hook,
For the night, in its own private Hinkle-Horn Nook.

All this long, happy day, they've been honking about
And the Hinkle-Horn Honkers have honked themselves out.
But they'll wake up quite fresh in the morning. And then . . .
They'll all start Hinkle-Horn honking again.

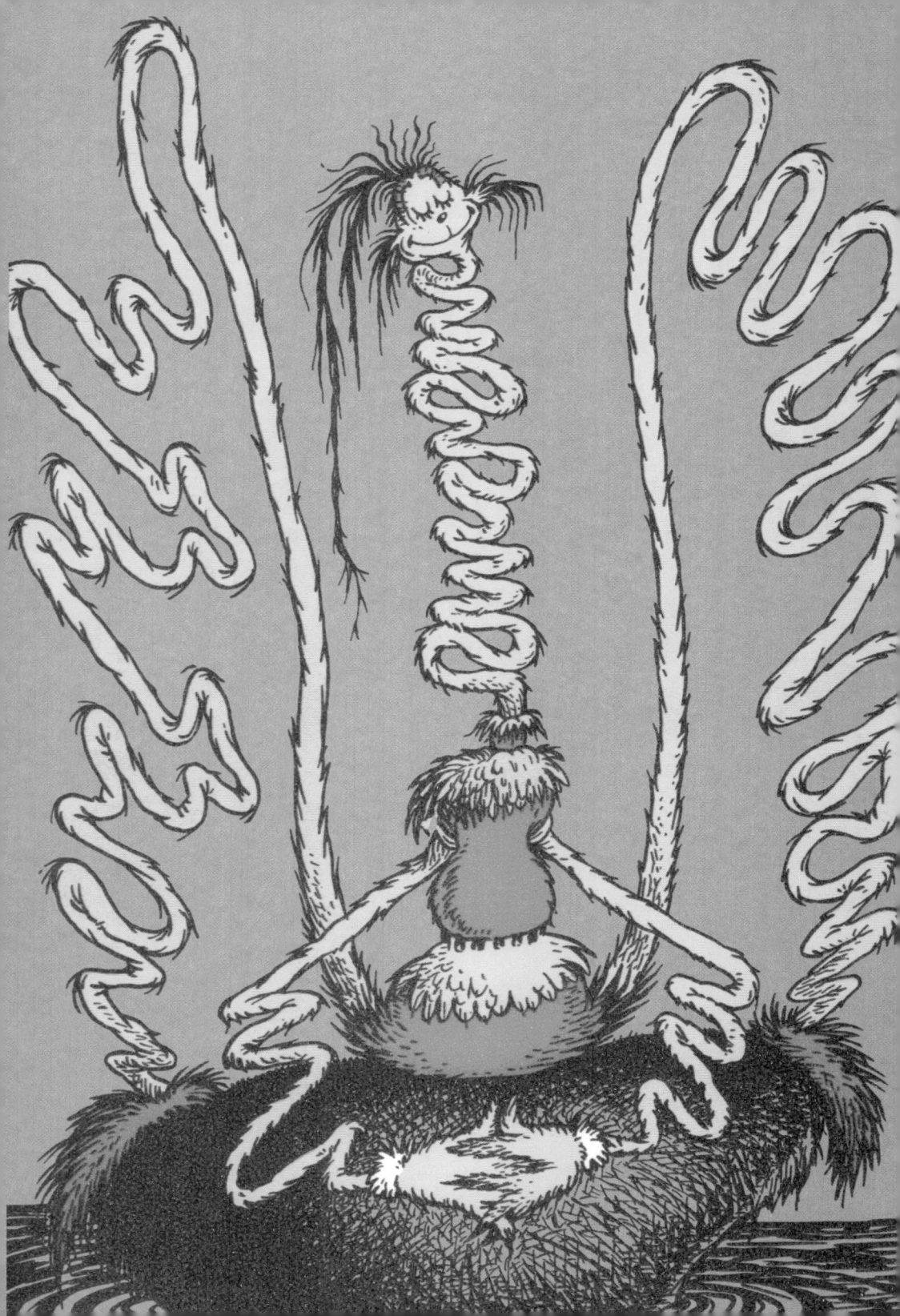

Everywhere, creatures
Are falling asleep.
The Collapsible Frink
Just collapsed in a heap.
And, by adding the Frink
To the others before,
I am able to give you
The Who's-Asleep-Score:
Right now, forty thousand
Four hundred and four
Creatures are happily,
Deeply in slumber.
I think you'll agree
That's a whopping fine number.

Counting up sleepers . . ?
Just how do we do it . . ?
Really quite simple. There's nothing much to it.
We find out how many, we learn the amount
By an Audio-Telly-o-Tally-o Count.
On a mountain, halfway between Reno and Rome,
We have a machine in a plexiglass dome
Which listens and looks into everyone's home.
And whenever it sees a new sleeper go flop,
It jiggles and lets a new Biggel-Ball drop.
Our chap counts these balls as they plup in a cup.
And that's how we know who is down and who's up.

KEEP OUT

Do you talk in your sleep . . ?
It's a wonderful sport
And I have some news of this sport to report.
The World-Champion Sleep-Talkers, Jo and Mo Redd-Zoff,
Have just gone to sleep and they're talking their heads off.
For fifty-five years, now, each chattering brother
Has babbled and gabbled all night to the other.

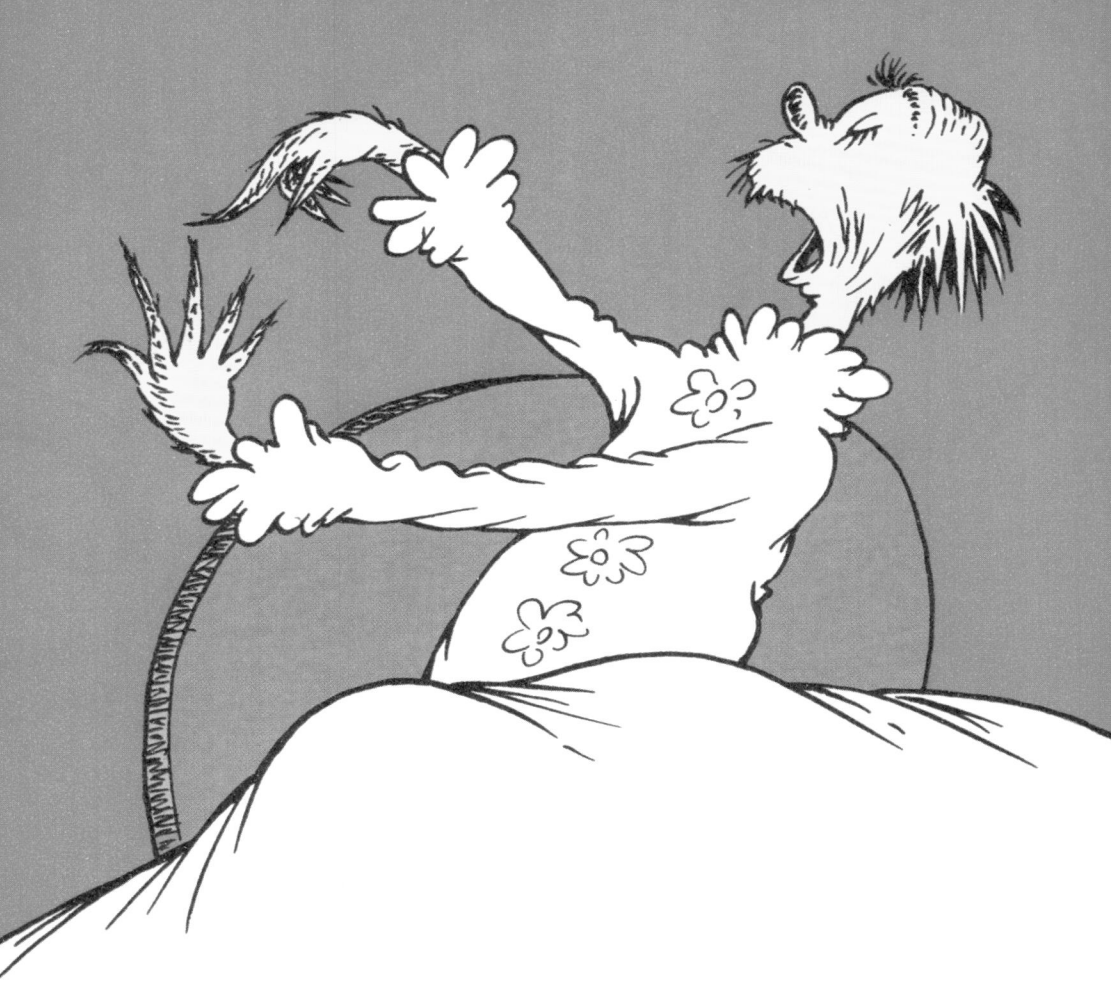

They've talked about laws and they've talked about gauze.
They've talked about paws and they've talked about flaws.
They've talked quite a lot about old Santa Claus.
And the reason I'm telling you this is because
You should take up this sport. It's just fine for the jaws.

Do you walk in your sleep . . ?
I just had a report
Of some interesting news of this popular sport.
Near Finnigan Fen, there's a sleepwalking group
Which not only walks, but it walks a-la-hoop!
Every night they go miles. Why, they walk to such length
They have to keep eating to keep up their strength.

So, every so often, one puts down his hoop,
Stops hooping and does some quick snooping for soup.
That's why they are known as the Hoop-Soup-Snoop Group.

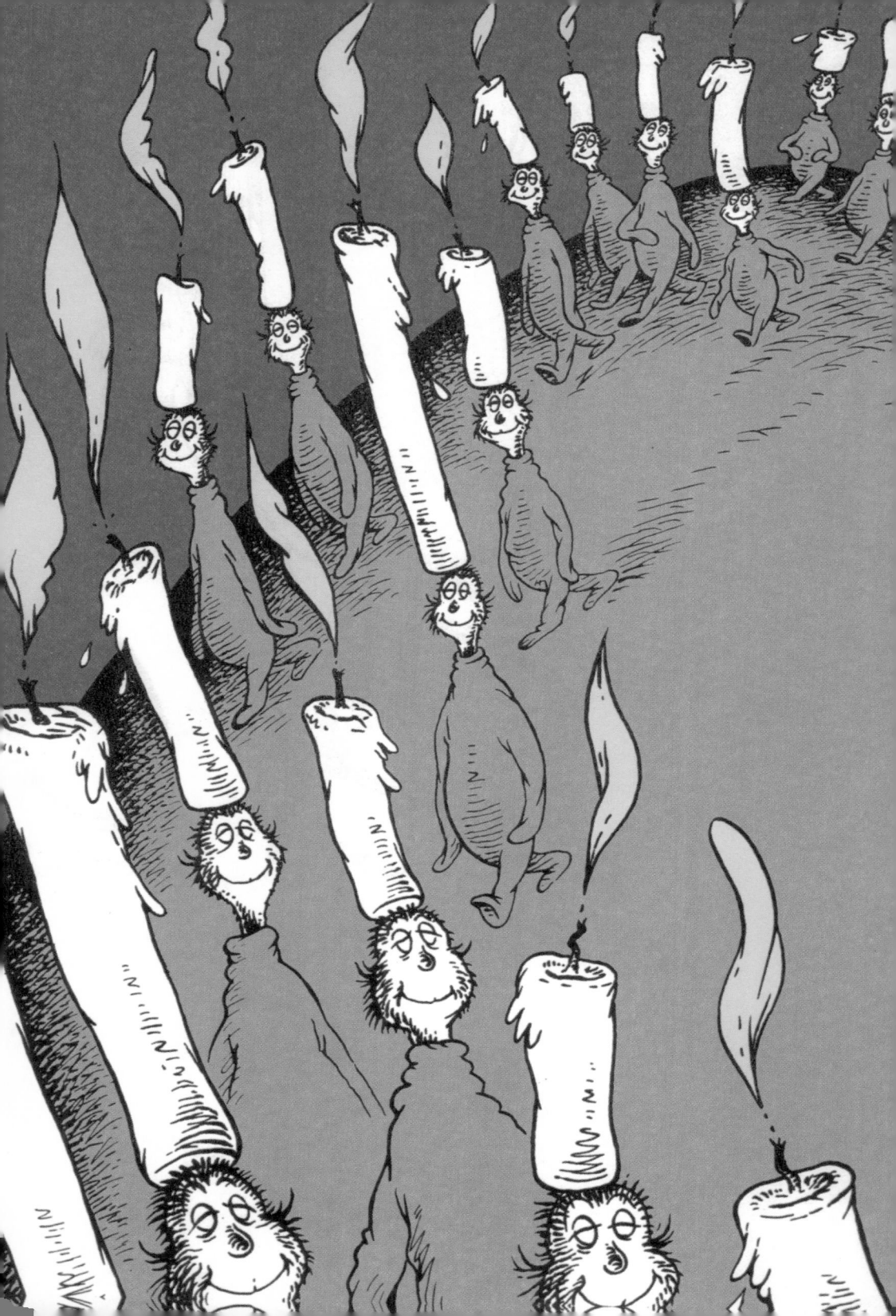

Sleepwalking, too, are the Curious Crandalls
Who sleepwalk on hills with assorted-sized candles.
The Crandalls walk nightly in slumbering peace
In spite of slight burns from the hot dripping grease.
The Crandalls wear candles because they walk far
And, it they wake up,
Want to see where they are.

Now the news has arrived
From the Valley of Vail
That a Chippendale Mupp has just bitten his tail,
Which he does every night before shutting his eyes.
Such nipping sounds silly. But, reall , it's wise.

He has no alarm clock. So this is the way
He makes sure that he'll wake at the right time of day.
His tail is so long, he won't feel any pain
'Til the nip makes the trip and gets up to his brain.
In exactly eight hours, the Chippendale Mupp
Will, at last, feel the bite and yell "Ouch!" and wake up.

A Mr. and Mrs. J. Carmichael Krox
Have just gone to bed near the town of Fort Knox.
And they, by the way, have the finest of clocks.

I'm not at all sure that I quite quite understand
Just how the thing works, with that one extra hand.
But I *do* know this clock does one very slick trick.
It doesn't tick tock. How it goes, is tock tick.
So, with ticks in its tocker, and tocks in its ticker
It saves lots of time and the sleepers sleep quicker.

What a fine night for sleeping! From all that I hear,
It's the best night for sleeping in many a year.
They're even asleep in the Zwieback Motel!
And people don't usually sleep there too well.

The beds are like rocks and, as everyone knows,
The sheets are too short. They won't cover your toes.
SO, if people are actually sleeping in THERE . . .
It's a great night for sleeping! It must be the air.

It's a great night for snores! I just had a report
Of some boys who are tops in this musical sport.
The snortiest snorers in all our fair land
Are Snorter McPhail and his Snore-a-Snort Band.
This band can snore *Dixie* and old *Swanee River*
So loud it would make forty elephants shiver.

The loudest of all of the boys is McPhail.
HE snores with his head in a three-gallon pail.
So they snore in a cave twenty miles out o f town.
If they snored closer in, they would snore the town down.

Do you know who's asleep
Out in Foona-Lagoona . . ?
Two very nice
Foona-Lagoona Baboona.

We've added them into our Who's-Asleep Count
Which has grown to a really amazing amount.
Exactly eight million, eight hundred and eight
Creatures are sleeping now! Isn't that great!

A Jedd is in bed,
And the bed of a Jedd
Is the softest
Of beds in the world,
It is said.
He makes it from pom poms
He grows on his head.
And he's sleeping right now
On the softest of fluff,
Completely exhausted
From growing the stuff.

The news has come in from the District of Dofft
That two Offt are asleep and they're sleeping aloft.
And how are they able to sleep off the ground . . ?
I'll tell you. I weighed one last week and I found
That an Offt is SO light he weighs minus one pound!

A moose is asleep.
He is dreaming of moose drinks.
A goose is asleep.
He is dreaming of goose drinks.
That's well and good when a moose dreams of moose juice.
And nothing goes wrong when a goose dreams of goose juic

But it isn't too good when a moose and a goose
Start dreaming they're drinking the other one's juice.
Moose juice, not goose juice, is juice for a moose
And goose juice, not moose juice, is juice for a goose.
So, when goose gets a mouthful of juices of moose's
And moose gets a mouthful of juices of goose's,
They always fall out of their beds screaming screams.
SO . . .
I'm warning you, now! Never drink in your dreams.

Speaking of dreaming,
I think you should note
That the Bumble-Tub Club Is now dreaming afloat.
Every night they go dreaming down Bumble-Tub Creek
Except for one night, every third or fourth week,
When they stop for repairs. 'Cause their bumble-tubs leak.
But tonight they're afloat, full of dreams, full of bliss,
And that's why I'm bothering telling you this.

At the fork of a road
In the Vale of Va-Vode
Five foot-weary salesmen have laid down their load.
All day they've raced round in the heat, at top speeds,
Unsuccessfully trying to sell Zizzer-Zoof Seeds
Which nobody wants because nobody needs.

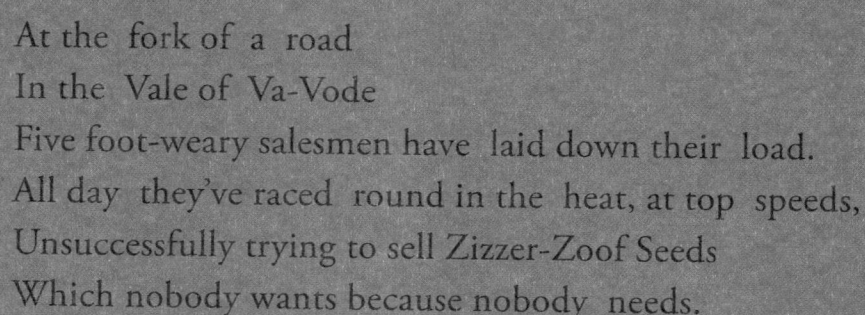

Tomorrow will come. They'll go back to their chore.
They'll start on the road, Zizzer-Zoofing once more
But tonight they've forgotten their feet are so sore.
And that's what the wonderful night time is for.

Everywhere,
Creatures
Have shut off their voices.
They've all gone to bed
In the beds of their choices.

They're sleeping in nooks.   And they're sleeping in cracks.
Some on their tummies, and some on their backs.
They're peacefully sleeping in comfortable holes.
Some, even, on soft-tufted barber shop poles.
The number of sleepers is now past the millions!
The number of sleepers is now in the billions!

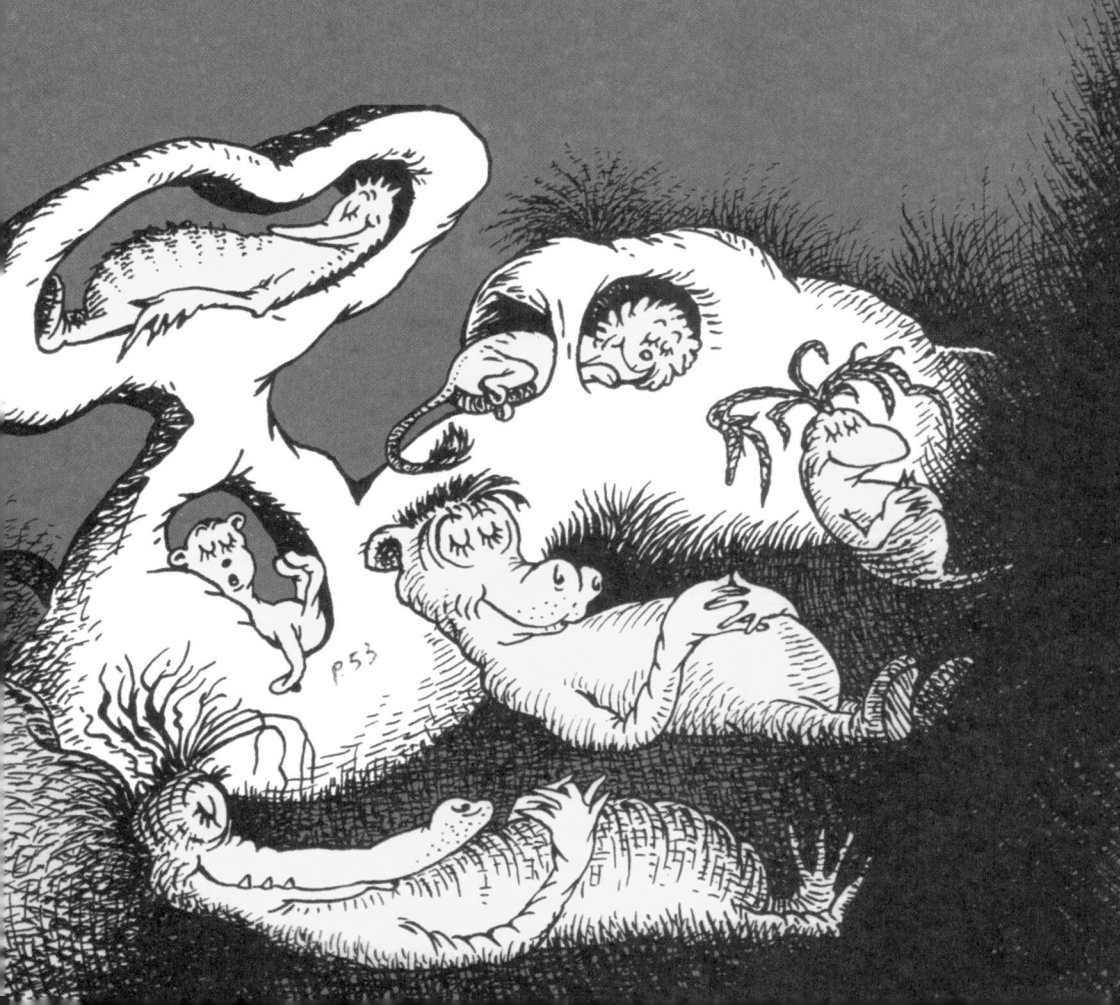

They're sleeping on steps! And on strings! And on floors!
In mailboxes, ships, and the keyholes of doors!
Every worm on a fishhook is safe for the night.
Every fish in the sea is too sleepy to bite.
Every whale in the ocean has turned off his spout.
Every light between here and Far Foodle is out.
And now, adding things up, we are way beyond billions!
Our Who's-Asleep-Score is now up in the Zillions!

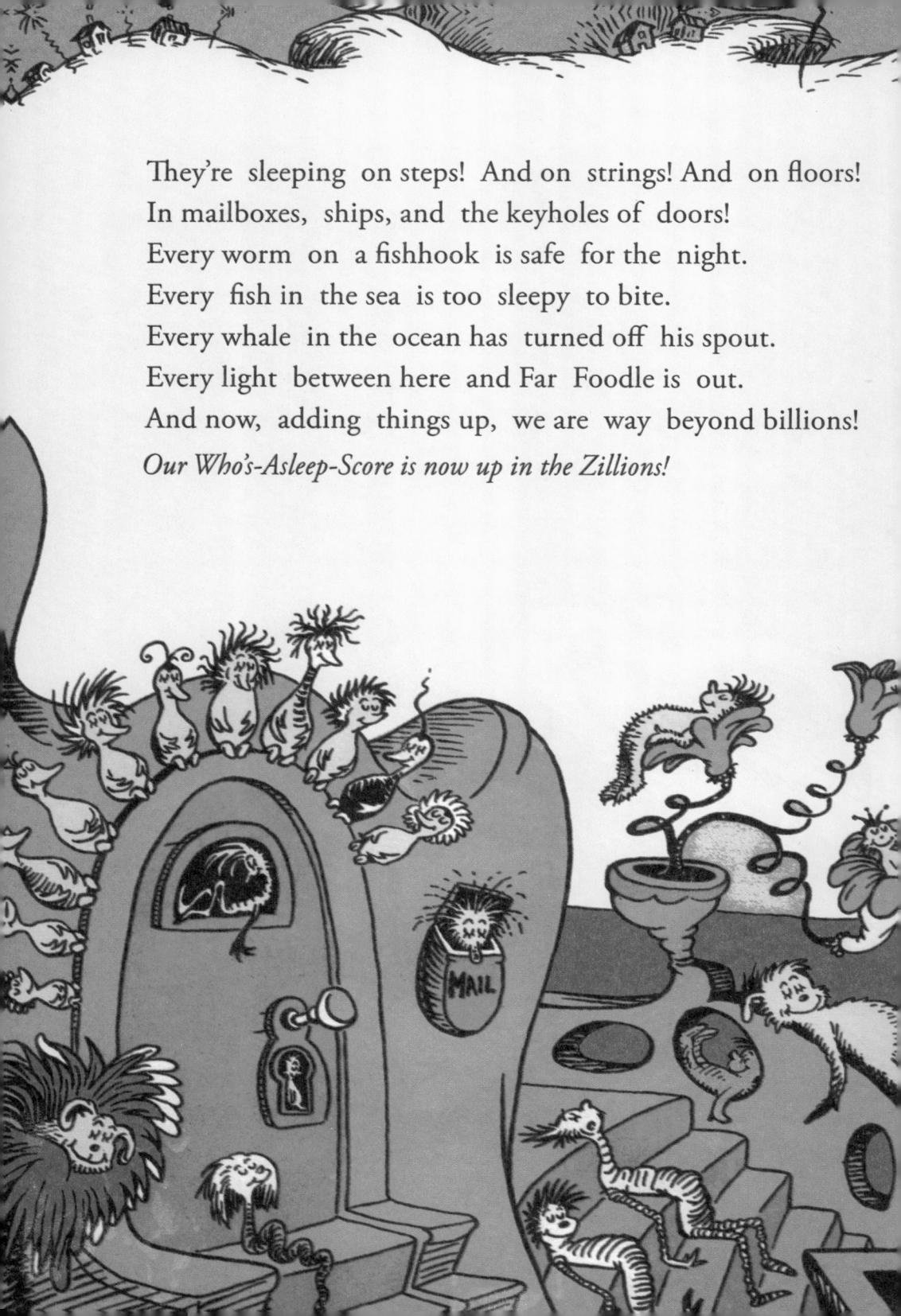

Ninety-nine zillion,
Nine trillion and two
Creatures are sleeping!
So . . .
How about you?

When you put out *your* light,
Then the number will be
Ninety-nine zillion
Nine trillion and three.

Good night.

ONE FISH TWO FISH
RED FISH BLUE FISH

By
Dr. Seuss

HarperCollins *Children's Books*

The Cat in the Hat
™ & © Dr. Seuss Enterprises, L.P. 1957
All Rights Reserved

3 5 7 9 10 8 6 4

ISBN 978-0-00-820149-4

© 1960, 1988 by Dr. Seuss Enterprises, L.P.
All Rights Reserved
A Beginner Book published by arrangement with
Random House Inc., New York, USA
First published in the UK 1960
This edition published in the UK 2016 by
HarperCollins *Children's Books,*
a division of HarperCollins*Publishers* Ltd
1 London Bridge Street
London SE1 9GF

Visit our website at:
www.harpercollins.co.uk

Printed and bound in India by Replika Press Pvt. Ltd.

From there to here,

from here to there,

funny things

are everywhere.

One fish

two fish

red fish

blue fish.

Black fish

blue fish

old fish

new fish.

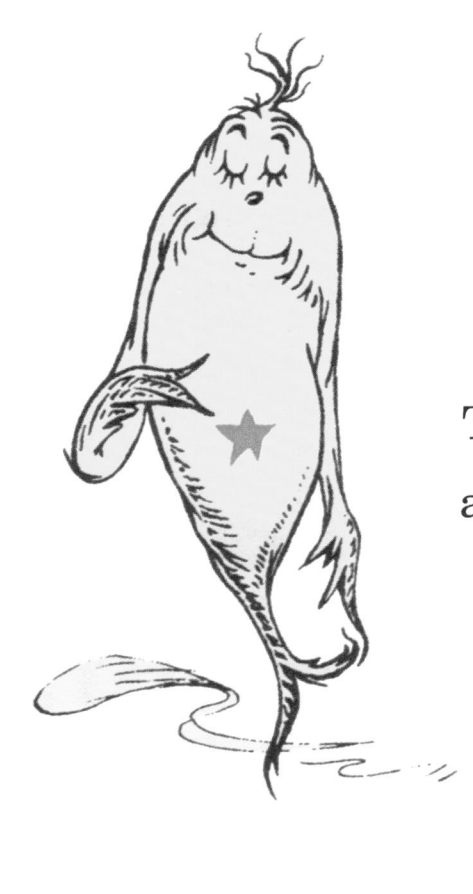

This one has
a little star.

This one has a little car.
Say! what a lot
of fish there are.

Yes. Some are red. And some are blue.
Some are old. And some are new.

Some are sad.

And some are glad.

And some are very, very bad.

Why are they
sad and glad and bad?
I do not know.
Go ask your dad.

Some are thin.

And some are fat.
The fat one has
a yellow hat.

8

From there to here,
from here to there,
funny things
are everywhere.

Here are some
who like to run.
They run for fun
in the hot, hot sun.

Oh me! Oh my!
Oh me! Oh my!
What a lot
of funny things go by.

Some have two feet
and some have four.
Some have six feet
and some have more.

Where do they come from? I can't say.

But I bet they have come

a long, long way.

We see them come.

We see them go.

Some are fast.

And some are slow.

Some are high.

And some are low.

Not one of them
is like another.
Don't ask us why.
Go ask your mother.

Say!

Look at his fingers!

One, two, three . . .

How many fingers

do I see?

One, two, three, four,

five, six, seven,

eight, nine, ten.

He has eleven!

Eleven!

This is something new.

I wish I had

eleven, too!

Bump!
Bump!
Bump!
Did you ever ride a Wump?
We have a Wump
with just one hump.

But

we know a man

called Mr. Gump.

Mr. Gump has a seven hump Wump.

So . . .

if you like to go Bump! Bump!

just jump on the hump of the Wump of Gump.

Who am I?

My name is Ned.

I do not like

my little bed.

This is no good.

This is not right.

My feet stick out

of bed all night.

And when I pull them in,
Oh, dear!
My head sticks out of bed
up here!

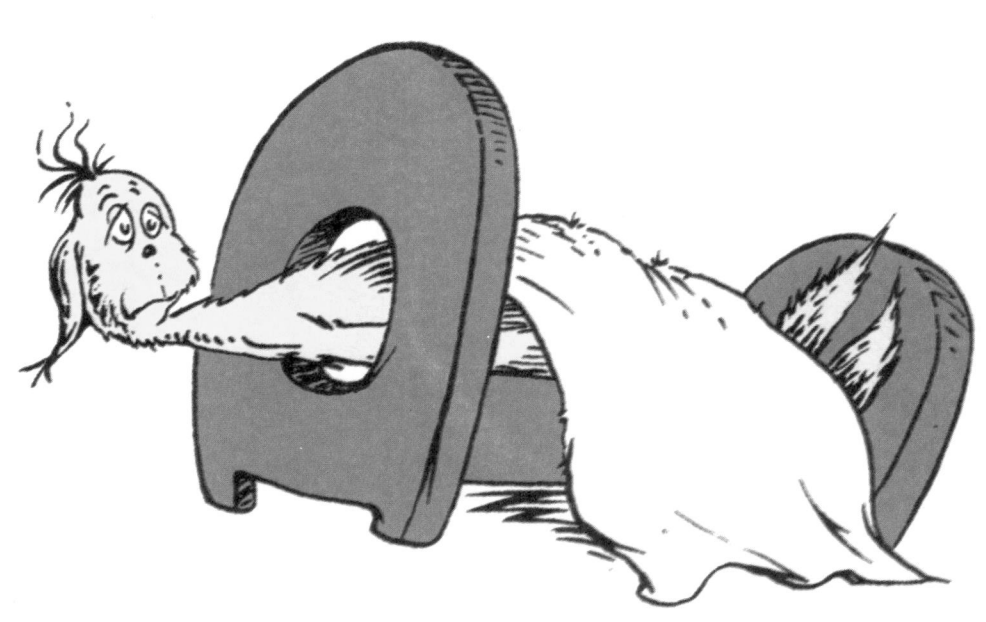

We like our bike.

It is made for three.

Our Mike

sits up in back,

you see.

22

We like our Mike
and this is why:
Mike does all the work
when the hills get high.

23

Hello there, Ned.
How do you do?
Tell me, tell me
what is new?
How are things
in your little bed?
What is new?
Please tell me, Ned.

I do not like
this bed at all.
A lot of things
have come to call.
A cow, a dog, a cat, a mouse.
Oh! what a bed! Oh! what a house!

Oh, dear! Oh, dear!
I can not hear.
Will you please
come over near?
Will you please look in my ear?
There must be something there, I fear.

Say, look!

A bird was in your ear.

But he is out. So have no fear.

Again your ear can hear, my dear.

My hat is old.
My teeth are gold.

I have a bird
I like to hold.

My shoe is off.
My foot is cold.

My shoe is off.
My foot is cold.

I have a bird
I like to hold.

My hat is old.
My teeth are gold.

And now
my story
is all told.

We took a look.
We saw a Nook.
On his head
he had a hook.
On his hook
he had a book.
On his book
was "How to Cook."

We saw him sit
and try to cook.
He took a look
at the book on the hook.

But a Nook can't read,
so a Nook can't cook.
SO . . .
what good to a Nook
is a hook cook book?

The moon was out
and we saw some sheep.
We saw some sheep
take a walk in their sleep.

By the light of the moon,
by the light of a star,
they walked all night
from near to far.

I would never walk.
I would take a car.

33

I do not like
this one so well.
All he does
is yell, yell, yell.
I will not have this one about.
When he comes in
I put him out.

This one is
quiet as a mouse.
I like to have him
in the house.

At our house
we open cans.
We have to open
many cans.
And that is why
we have a Zans.

A Zans for cans
is very good.
Have you a Zans for cans?
You should.

I like to box.

How I like to box!

So, every day,

I box a Gox.

38

In yellow socks
I box my Gox.
I box in yellow
Gox box socks.

It is fun to sing
if you sing with a Ying.
My Ying can sing
like anythings.

I sing high
and my Ying sings low,
and we are not too bad,
you know.

This one,
I think,
is called
a Yink.

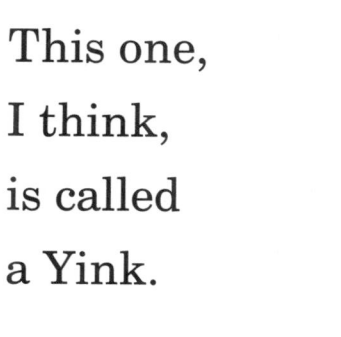

He likes to wink,

he likes to drink.

He likes to drink, and drink, and drink.
The thing he likes to drink
is ink.
The ink he likes to drink is pink.
He likes to wink and drink pink ink.

SO . . .
if you have a lot of ink,
then you should get
a Yink, I think.

Hop! Hop! Hop!
I am a Yop.
All I like to do is hop
from finger top
to finger top.

I hop from left to right
and then . . .
Hop! Hop!
I hop right back again.

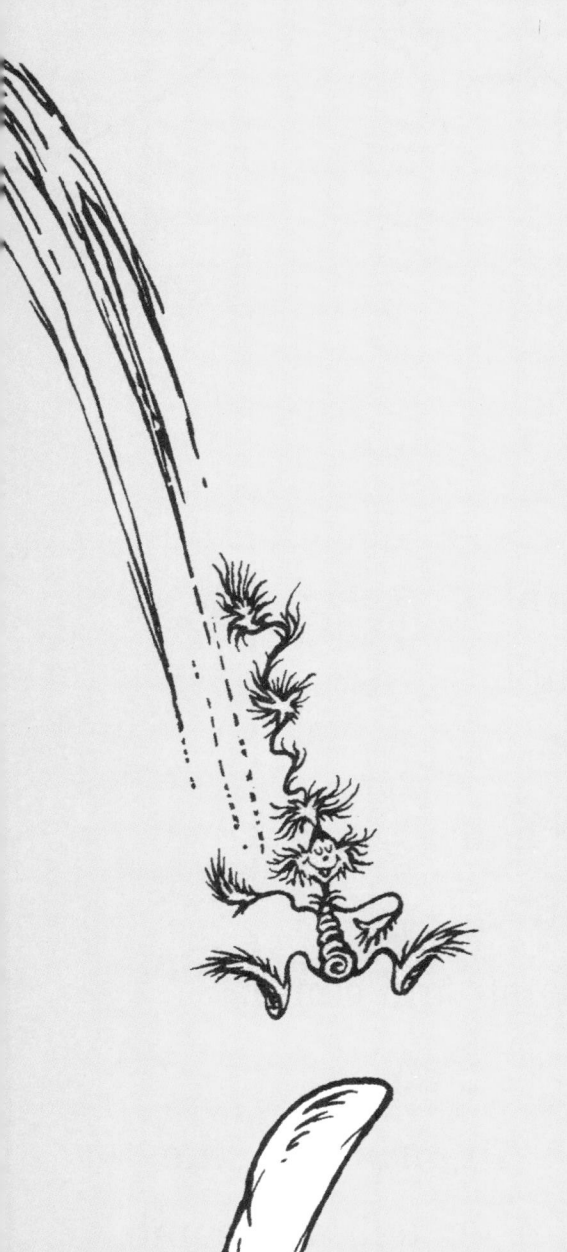

I like to hop
all day and night
from right to left
and left to right.

Why do I like to
hop, hop, hop?
I do not know.
Go ask your Pop.

45

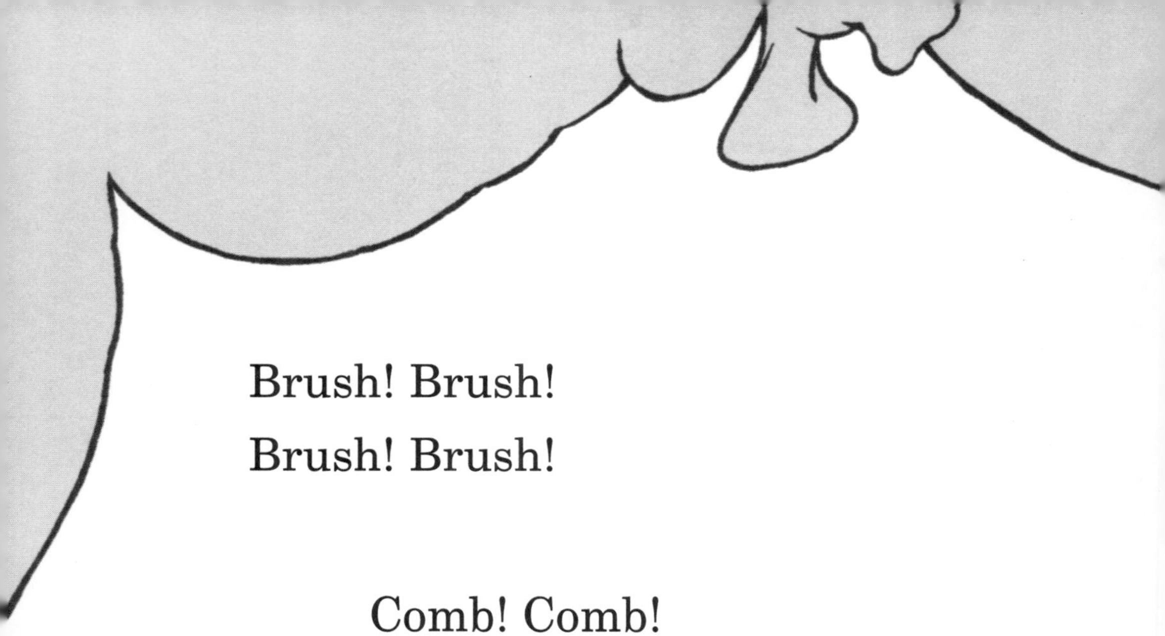

Brush! Brush!
Brush! Brush!

Comb! Comb!
Comb! Comb!

Blue hair
is fun
to brush and comb.

All girls who like
to brush and comb
should have a pet
like this at home.

Who is this pet?

Say!

He is wet.

You never yet

met a pet,

I bet,

as wet as they let

this wet pet get.

Did you ever
fly a kite
in bed?

Did you ever walk
with ten cats
on your head?

Did you ever milk
this kind of cow?
Well, we can do it.
We know how.

If you never did,
you should.
These things are fun
and fun is good.

Hello!
Hello!
Are you there?
Hello!
I called you up
to say hello.
I said hello.
Can you hear me, Joe?

Oh, no.

I can not hear your call.

I can not hear your call at all.

This is not good

and I know why.

A mouse has cut the wire.

Good-bye!

From near to far
from here to there,
funny things are everywhere.

These yellow pets
are called the Zeds.
They have one hair
up on their heads.
Their hair grows fast . . .
so fast, they say,
they need a hair cut
every day.

Who am I?

My name is Ish.

On my hand I have a dish.

I have this dish
to help me wish.

When I wish to make a wish
I wave my hand with a big swish swish.
Then I say, "I wish for fish!"
And I get fish right on my dish.

So . . .

if you wish to wish a wish,
you may swish for fish
with my Ish wish dish.

At our house
we play out back.
We play a game
called Ring the Gack.

Would you like to play this game?
Come down!
We have the only
Gack in town.

Look what we found
in the park
in the dark.
We will take him home.
We will call him Clark.

He will live at our house.
He will grow and grow.
Will our mother like this?
We don't know.

And now
good night.
It is time to sleep.
So we will sleep
with our pet Zeep.

Today is gone. Today was fun.

Tomorrow is another one.

Every day,

from here to there,

funny things are everywhere.

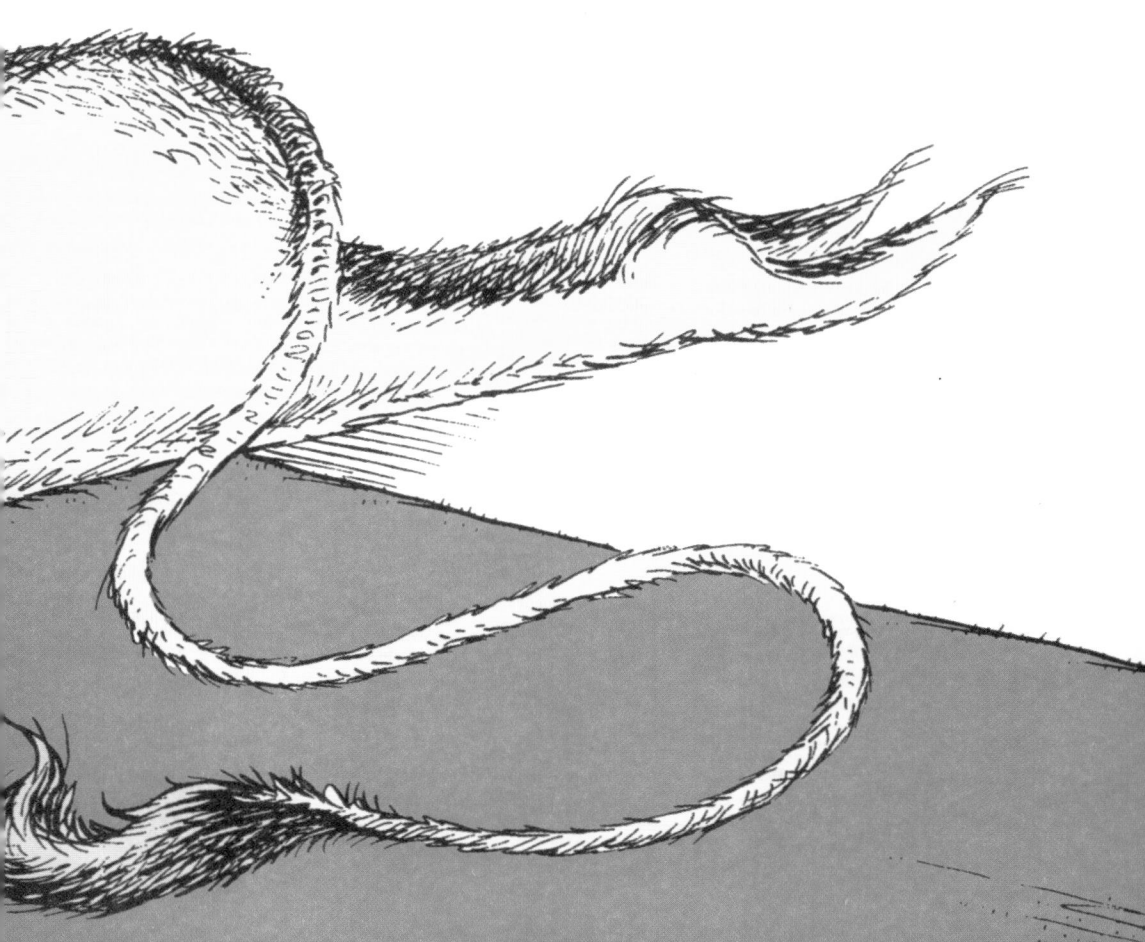

Dr. Seuss's ABC

By
Dr. Seuss

HarperCollins *Children's Books*

™ & © Dr. Seuss Enterprises, L.P. 1957
All Rights Reserved

A CIP catalogue record for this title is available from
the British Library.
No part of this publication may be reproduced, stored
in a retrieval system or transmitted in any form or by
any means, electronic, mechanical, photocopying,
recording or otherwise, without the prior permission of
HarperCollins Publishers Ltd, 1 London Bridge Street
London SE1 9GF

3 5 7 9 10 8 6 4

ISBN 978-0-00-820391-7

© 1963, 1991 by Dr. Seuss Enterprises, L.P.
All Rights Reserved
Published by arrangement with
Random House Inc., New York, USA
First published in the UK 1964
This edition published in the UK 2017 by
HarperCollins *Children's Books,*
a division of HarperCollins*Publishers* Ltd
1 London Bridge Street
London SE1 9GF

Visit our website at:
www.harpercollins.co.uk

Printed and bound in India by Replika Press Pvt. Ltd.

This book is produced from independently certified FSC® paper
to ensure responsible forest management.

BIG A

little   a

What begins with A ?

Aunt Annie's alligator .

. . . . A . . a . . A

BIG B
little   b

What begins with B ?

Barber
baby
bubbles
and a
bumblebee.

9

BIG C

little   c

What begins with C?

Camel on the ceiling
C . . . . c C

11

BIG D

little   d

David Donald Doo
dreamed
a dozen doughnuts
and
a duck-dog, too.

ABCDE..e..e

ear

egg

elephant

e

e

E

13

ABCDE . . e . . e

ear

egg

elephant

e

e

E

BIG F
little   f

F .. f .. F

Four fluffy feathers
on a
Fiffer-feffer-feff.

17

ABCD
EFG

Goat
girl
googoo goggles
G . . . g . . . G

BIG H

little h

Hungry horse.
Hay.

Hen in a hat.
Hooray !
Hooray !

BIG I
little   i

i . . . . i i

Icabod
is
itchy.

So am I.

BIG J
little   j

What begins with j?

Jerry Jordan's
jelly jar
and jam
begin that way.

BIG K

little   k

Kitten. Kangaroo.

Kick a kettle.
Kite
and a
king's kerchoo.

BIG L

Little Lola Lopp.
Left leg.
Lazy lion
licks a lollipop.

29

BIG M

little   m

Many mumbling mice
are making
midnight music
in the moonlight . . .

mighty nice

31

BIG N

little   n

What begins with those ?

Nine new neckties
and a nightshirt
and a nose.

33

O is very useful.
   You use it when you say:
"Oscar's only ostrich
   oiled
   an orange owl today."

35

ABCD
EFG
HIJK
LMNO.

...P

37

Painting pink pyjamas.
Policeman in a pail.

Peter Pepper's puppy.
And now
Papa's in the pail.

BIG Q

little   q

What begins with Q ?

The quick
Queen of Quincy
and her
quacking quacker-oo.

QUACK
QUACK

41

BIG R

little   r

Rosy Robin Ross.

Rosy's going riding
on her
red rhinoceros.

BIG S

little s

Silly Sammy Slick
sipped six sodas
and got
sick sick sick.

45

T . . . . . T

t . . . . t

What begins with T ?

Ten tired turtles
on a tuttle-tuttle tree.

47

BIG U

little   u

What begins with U ?

Uncle Ubb's umbrella
and his
underwear, too.

49

BIG V

little   v

Vera Violet Vinn
is
very
very
very awful
on her violin.

51

W . . w . . W

Willy Waterloo
washes Warren Wiggins
who is
washing Waldo Woo.

X is very useful
if your name is
Nixie Knox.
It also
comes in handy
spelling axe
and extra fox.

NIXIE KNOX

55

BIG Y
little y

A yawning yellow yak.
Young Yolanda Yorgenson
is yelling on his back.

58

BIG Z
little   z

What begins with Z ?

I do.

I am a
Zizzer-Zazzer-Zuzz
as you can
plainly see.

TEN APPLES UP ON TOP

By
Dr. Seuss

writing as

Theo. LeSieg

Illustrated by Roy McKie

HarperCollins *Children's Books*

HarperCollins
PUBLISHERS
Since 1817

™ & © Dr. Seuss Enterprises, L.P.
All Rights Reserved

A CIP catalogue record for this title is available from the
British Library.
No part of this publication may be reproduced, stored
in a retrieval system or transmitted in any form or by
any means, electronic, mechanical, photocopying,
recording or otherwise, without the prior permission of
HarperCollins Publishers Ltd, 1 London Bridge Street
London SE1 9GF

3 5 7 9 10 8 6 4

ISBN 978-0-00-823999-2

© 1961 by Random House, Inc.
™ & © renewed 1989 by Dr. Seuss Enterprises, L.P.
and Roy McKie
All Rights Reserved
Published by arrangement with Random House Inc.,
New York, USA
First published in the UK 1963
This edition published in the UK 2017 by
HarperCollins *Children's Books,*
a division of HarperCollins*Publishers* Ltd
1 London Bridge Street
London SE1 9GF

www.harpercollins.co.uk

Printed and bound in India by Replika Press Pvt. Ltd.

MIX
Paper from
responsible sources
FSC® C016779

This book is produced from independently certified FSC® paper
to ensure responsible forest management.

One apple
up on top!

3

Two apples
up on top!

4

Look, you.
I can do it, too.

Look!

See!

I can do three!

Three . . .

Three . . .

    I see.

      I see.

You can do three
but I can do more.
You have three
but I have four.

Look! See, now.
I can hop
with four apples
up on top.

13

And I can hop
up on a tree
with four apples
up on me.

Look here, you two.

See here, you two.

I can get five

on top.

Can you?

I am so good
I will not stop.
Five!
Now six!
Now seven on top!

Seven apples
up on top!

20

I am
so good
they will not drop.

Five, six, seven!
Fun, fun, fun!
Seven, six, five,
four, three, two, one!

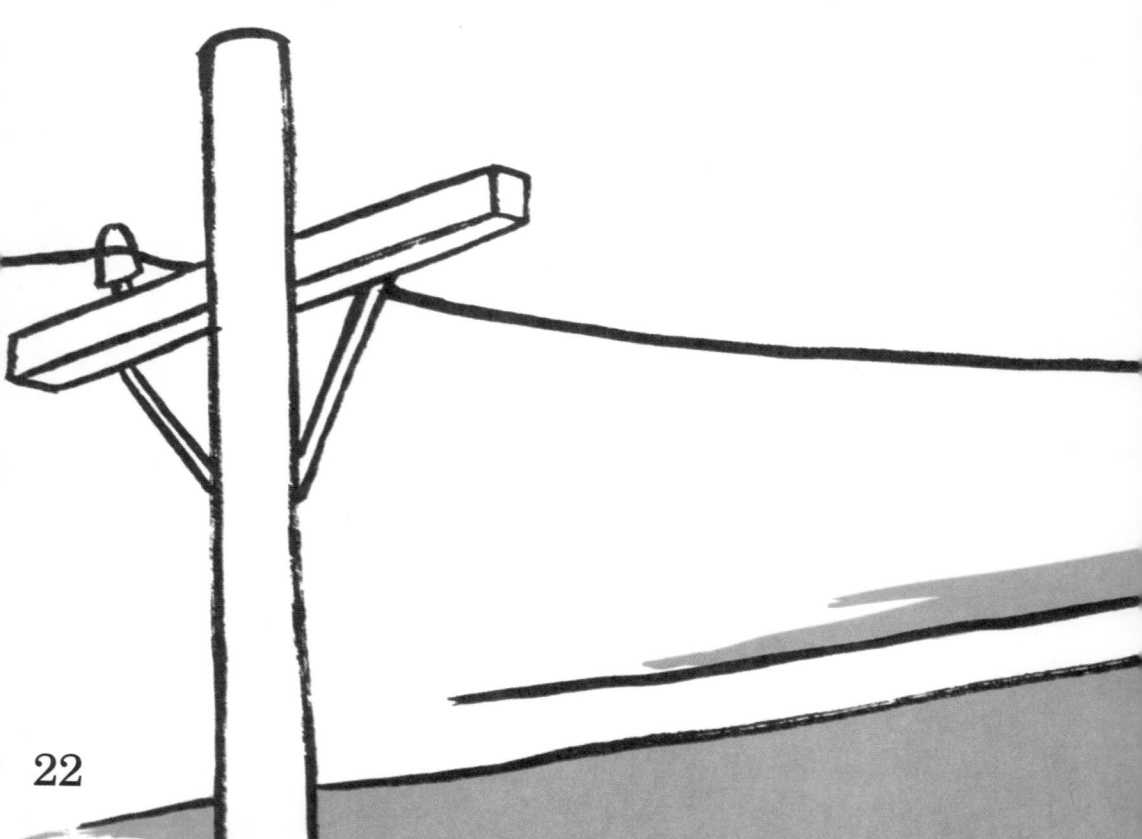

But, see!
We are as good as you.
Look! Now we
have seven, too.

And now, see here.

Eigth! Eight on top!

Eight apples up!

Not one will drop.

Eight! Eight!
And we can skate.
Look now!
We can skate
with eight.

29

But I can do nine.
And hop!
And drink!
You can not do this,
I think.

We can! We can!

We can do it, too.

See here.

We are as good as you!

We all are very good
I think.
With nine we all
can hop and drink.

Nine is very good.
But then . . .
Come on and we
will make it ten!

Look!

Ten

apples

up

on

top!

We are not

going to let them drop!

Look out!
Look out!
I see a mop.

I will make
the apples fall.
Get out. Get out. You!
One and all!

Come on! Come on!
Come down this hall.
We must not let
our apples fall!

43

44

Out of our way!
We can not stop.
We can not let
our apples drop.

This is not good.
What will we do?
They want to get
our apples, too.

48

They will get them
if we let them.
Come! We can not
let them get them.

Look out!

The mop!

The mop!

The mop!

You can not stop
our apple fun.
Our apples will not drop.
Not one!

53

Come on! Come on!
Come one! Come all!
We have to make
the apples fall.

They must not get
our apples down.
Come on! Come on!
Get out of town!

Apples!
Apples up on top!
All of this
must stop
STOP
STOP!

Now all our fun
is going to stop!
Our apples all
are going to drop.

59

What fun!
We will not
let them fall.

THE CAT IN THE HAT

By

Dr. Seuss

HarperCollins *Children's Books*

The sun did no shine.

It was too wet to play.

So we sat in the house

All that cold, cold, wet day.

I sat there with Sally.

We sat there, we two.

And I said, "How I wish

We had something to do!"

Too wet to go out

And too cold to play ball.

So we sat in the house.

We did nothing at all.

So all we could do was to
Sit!
   Sit!
      Sit!
         Sit!
And we did not like it.
Not one little bit.

And then

Something went BUMP!

How that bump made us jump!

We looked!

Then we saw him step in on the mat!

We looked!

And we saw him!

The Cat in the Hat!

And he said to us,

"Why do you sit there like that?"

"I know it is wet

And the sun is not sunny.

But we can have

Lots of good fun that is funny!"

"I know some good games we could play,"

Said the cat.

"I know some new tricks,"

Said the Cat in the Hat.

"A lot of good tricks.

I will show them to you.

Your mother

Will not mind at all if I do."

Then Sally and I

Did not know what to say.

Our mother was out of the house

For the day.

But our fish said, "No! No!
Make that cat go away!
Tell that Cat in the Hat
You do NOT want to play.
He should not be here.
He should not be about.
He should not be here
When your mother is out!"

"Now! Now! Have no fear.
Have no fear!" said the cat.
"My tricks are not bad,"
Said the Cat in the Hat.
"Why, we can have
Lots of good fun, if you wish,
With a game that I call
Up-up-up with a fish!"

"Put me down!" said the fish.
"This is no fun at all!
Put me down!" said the fish.
"I do NOT wish to fall!"

"Have no fear!" said the cat.

"I will not let you fall.

I will hold you up high

As I stand on a ball.

With a book on one hand!

And a cup on my hat!

But that is not ALL I can do!"

Said the cat. . .

"Look at me!

Look at me now!" said the cat.

"With a cup and a cake

On the top of my hat!

I can hold up TWO books!

I can hold up the fish!

And a little toy ship!

And some milk on a dish!

And look!

I can hop up and down on the ball!

But that is not all!

Oh, no.

That is not all . . .

"Look at me!

Look at me!

Look at me NOW!

It is fun to have fun

But you have to know how.

I can hold up the cup

And the milk and the cake!

I can hold up these books!

And the fish on a rake!

I can hold the toy ship

And a little toy man!

And look! With my tail

I can hold a red fan!

I can fan with the fan

As I hop on the ball!

But that is not all.

Oh, no.

That is not all. . . ."

That is what the cat said . . .
Then he fell on his head!
He came down with a bump
From up there on the ball.
And Sally and I,
We saw ALL the things fall!

And our fish came down, too.

He fell into a pot!

He said, "Do I like this?

Oh, no! I do not.

This is not a good game,"

Said our fish as he lit.

"No, I do not like it,

Not one little bit!"

"Now look what you did!"

Said the fish to the cat.

"Now look at this house!

Look at this! Look at that!

You sank our toy ship,

Sank it deep in the cake.

You shook up our house

And you bent our new rake

You SHOULD NOT be here

When our mother is not.

You get out of this house!"

Said the fish in the pot.

"But I like to be here.

Oh, I like it a lot!"

Said the Cat in the Hat

To the fish in the pot.

"I will NOT go away.

I do NOT wish to go!

And so," said the Cat in the Hat,

"So

    so

      so . . .

I will show you

Another good game that I know!"

And then he ran out.

And, then, fast as a fox,

The Cat in the Hat

Came back in with a box.

A big red wood box.

It was shut with a hook.

"Now look at this trick,"

Said the cat.

"Take a look!"

Then he got up on top

With a tip of his hat.

"I call this game FUN-IN A BOX,"

Said the cat.

"In this box are two things

I will show to you now.

You will like these two things,"

Said the cat with a bow.

"I will pick up the hook.

You will see something new.

Tow things. And I call them

Thing One and Thing Two.

These Things will not bite you.

They want to have fun."

Then, out of the box

Came Thing Two and Thing One!

And they ran to us fast.

They said, "How do you do?

Would you like to shake hands

With Thing One and Thing Two?"

And Sally and I
Did not know what to do.
So we had to shake hands
With Thing One and Thing Two.
We shook their two hands.
But our fish said, "No! No!
Those Things should not be
In this house! Make them go!

"They should not be here
When your mother is not!
Put them out! Put them out!"
Said the fish in the pot.

"Have no fear, little fish,"
Said the Cat in the Hat.
"These Things are good Things."
And he gave them a pat.
"They are tame. Oh, so tame!
They have come here to play.
They will give you some fun
On this wet, wet, wet day."

"Now, here is a game that they like,"
Said the cat.
"They like to fly kites,"
Said the Cat in the Hat.

"No!   Not in the house!"
Said the fish in the pot.
"They should not fly kites
In a house! They should not.
Oh, the things they will bump!
Oh, the things they will hit!
Oh, I do not like it!
Not one little bit!"

Then Sally and I
Saw them run down the hall.
We saw those two Things
Bump their kites on the wall!
Bump! Thump! Thump! Bump!
Down the wall in the hall.

Thing Two and Thing One!

They ran up! They ran down!

On the string of one kite

We saw Mother's new gown!

Her gown with the dots

That are pink, white and red.

Then we saw one kite bump

On the head of her bed!

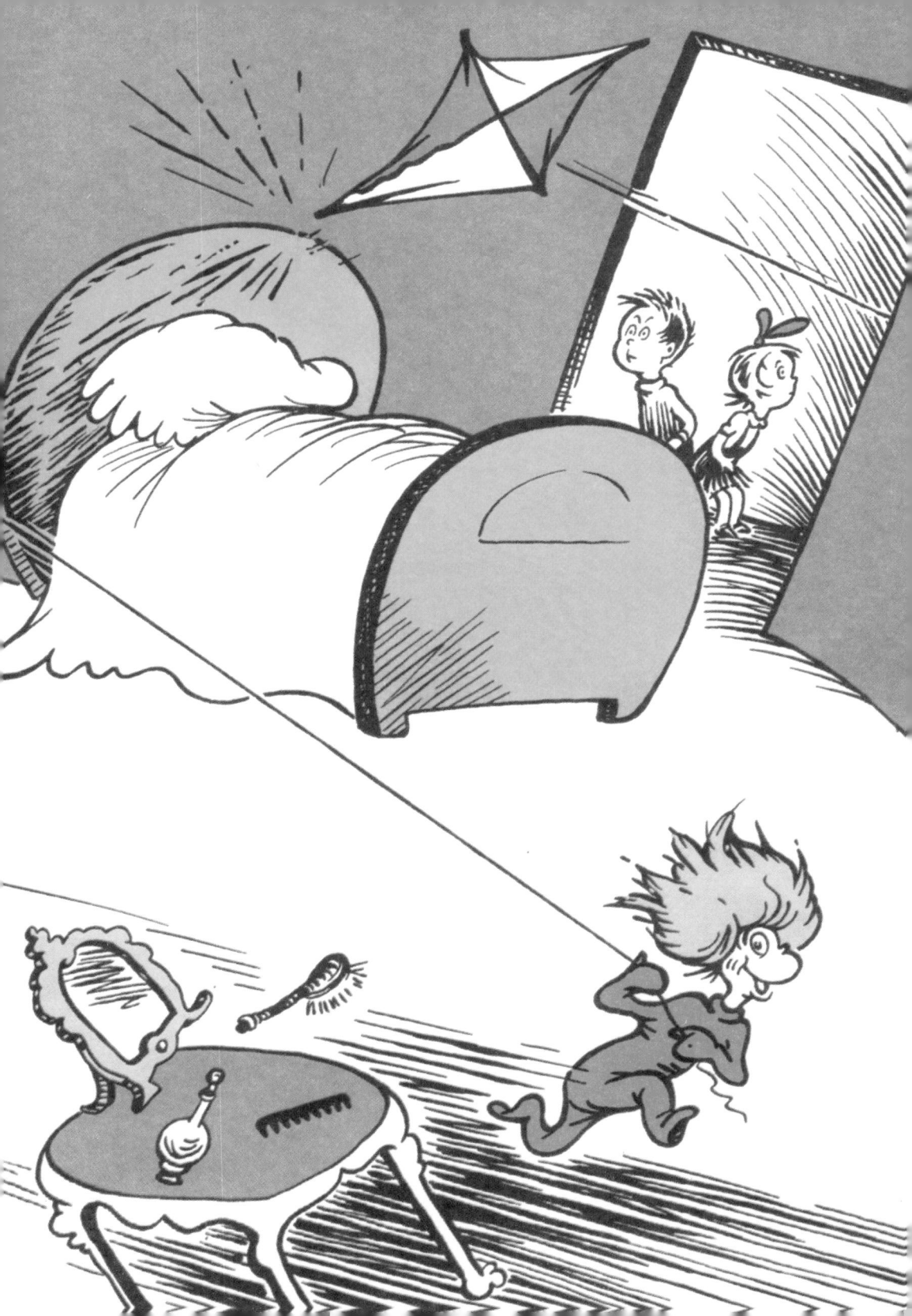

Then those Things ran about

With big bumps, jumps and kicks

And with hops and big thumps

And all kinds of bad tricks.

And I said,

"I do NOT like the way that they play!

If Mother could see this,

Oh, what would she say!"

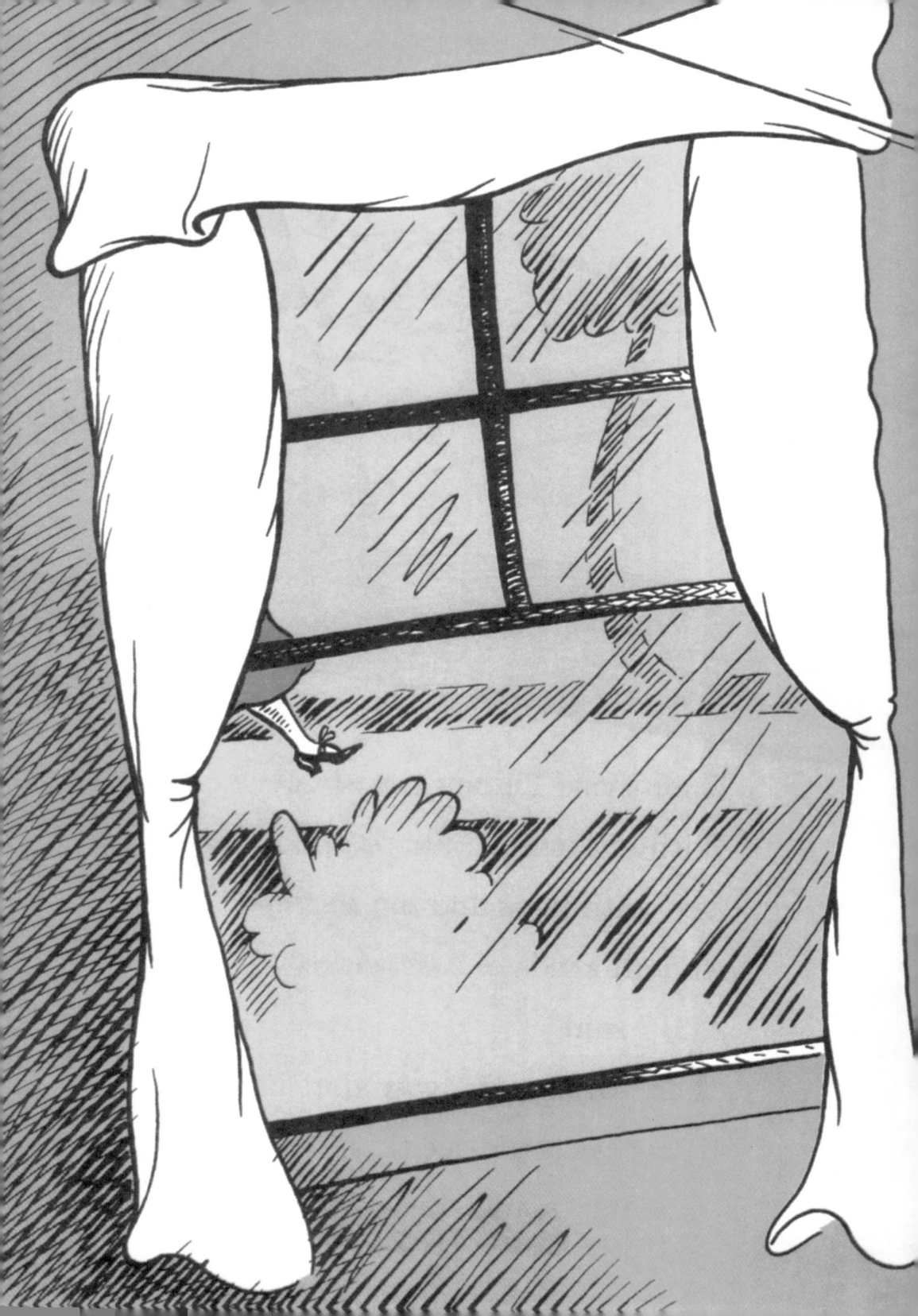

Then our fish said, "Look! Look!"
And our fish shook with fear.
"Your mother is on her way home!
Do you hear?
Oh, what will she do to us?
What will she say?
Oh, she will not like it
To find us this way!"

"So, DO something! Fast!" said the fish.

"Do you hear!

I saw her.   Your mother!

Your mother is near!

So, as fast as you can,

Think of something to do!

You will have to get rid of

Thing One and Thing Two!"

So, as fast as I could,
I went after my net.
And I said, "With my net
I can get them I bet.
I bet, with my net,
I can get those Things Yet!"

Then I let down my net.

It came down with a PLOP!

And I had them! At last!

Those tow Things had to stop.

Then I said to the cat,

"Now you do as I say.

You pack up those Things

And you take them away!"

"Oh dear!" said the cat.

"You did not like our game . . .

Oh dear.

What a shame!

What a shame!

What a shame!"

Then he shut up the Things
In the box with the hook.
And the cat went away
With a sad kind of look.

"That is good," said the fish.

"He has gone away.   Yes.

But your mother will come.

She will find this big meas!

And this mess is so big

And so deep and so tall,

We can not pick it up.

There is no way at all!"

And THEN!

Who was back in the house?

Why, the cat!

"Have no fear of this mess,"

Said the Cat in the Hat.

"I always pick up all my playthings

And so . . .

I will show you another

Good trick that I know!"

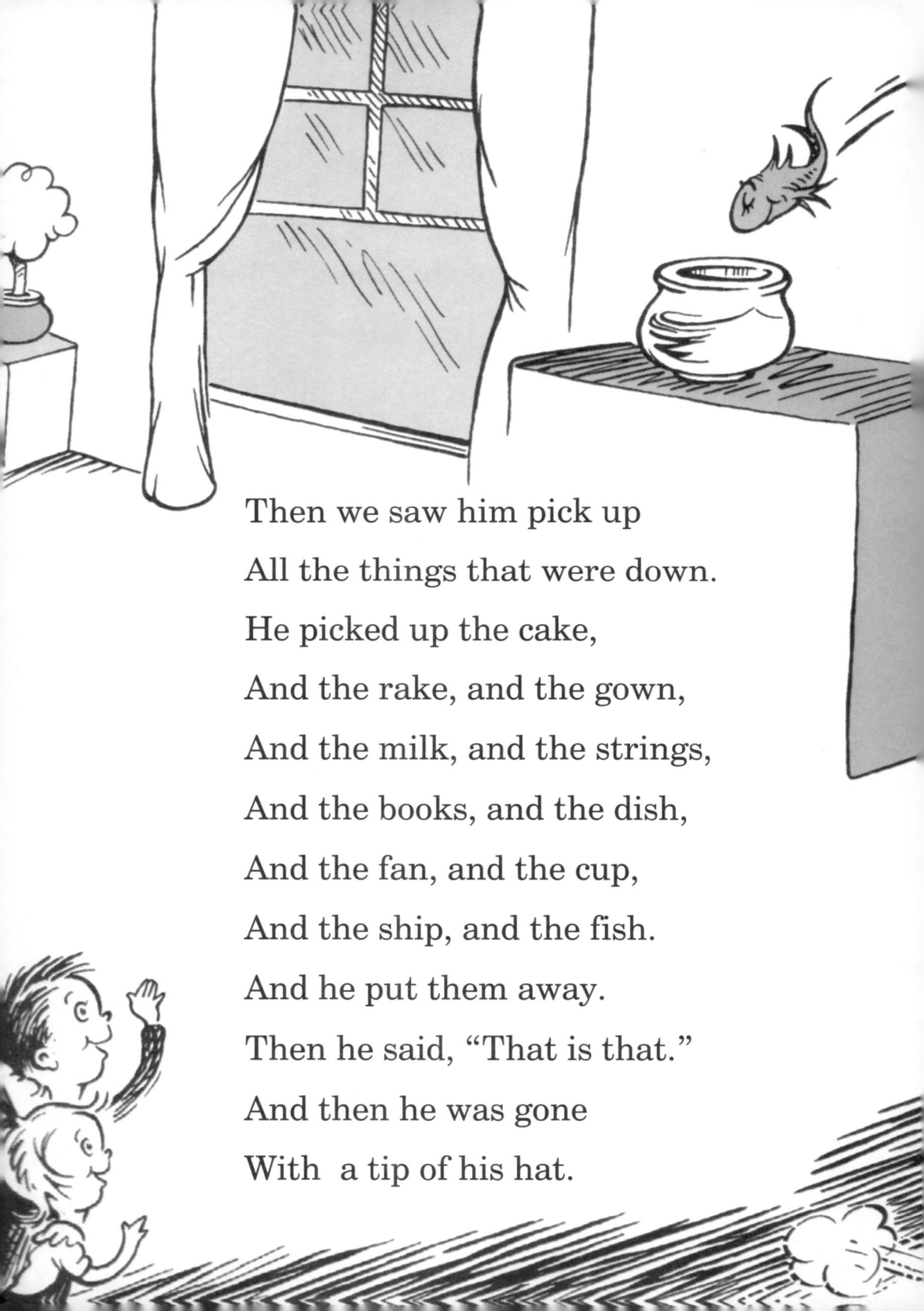

Then we saw him pick up

All the things that were down.

He picked up the cake,

And the rake, and the gown,

And the milk, and the strings,

And the books, and the dish,

And the fan, and the cup,

And the ship, and the fish.

And he put them away.

Then he said, "That is that."

And then he was gone

With a tip of his hat.

Then our mother came in
And she said to us two,
"Did you have any fun?
Tell me. What did you do?"

And Sally and I did not know
What to say.
Should we tell her
The things that went on there that day?

Should we tell her about it?

Now, what SHOULD we do?

Well . . .

What would YOU do

If your mother asked YOU?

THERE'S A WOCKET IN MY POCKET!

By

Dr. Seuss

HarperCollins *Children's Books*

And a
FINDOW
in my
WINDOW

The Cat in the Hat
™ & © Dr. Seuss Enterprises, L.P. 1957
All Rights Reserved

A CIP catalogue record for this title is available from the
British Library.

3 5 7 9 10 8 6 4

ISBN 978-0-00-823998-5

© 1974, 2002 by Dr. Seuss Enterprises, L.P.
All Rights Reserved
A Bright and Early Book for Beginning Beginners,
published by arrangement with Random House Inc.,
New York, USA
First published in the UK 1975
This edition published in the UK 2017 by
HarperCollins *Children's Books,*
a division of HarperCollins*Publishers* Ltd
1 London Bridge Street
London SE1 9GF

www.harpercollins.co.uk

Printed and bound in India by Replika Press Pvt. Ltd.

This book is produced from independently certified FSC®paper
to ensure responsible forest management.

Did you
ever have the feeling
there's a
WASKET
in your
BASKET?

. . .Or a NUREAU
in your BUREAU?

. . . Or a WOSET in your CLOSET?

Sometimes
I feel quite CERTAIN
there's a JERTAIN
in the CURTAIN.

Sometimes
I have the feeling
there's a ZLOCK
behind the CLOCK.

And that ZELF
up on that SHELF!

I have
talked to him
myself.

That's the
kind of house
I live in.

There's a NINK
in the SINK.

And a
ZAMP
in the
LAMP.

And they're
rather nice
. . . I think.

Some of them
are very friendly.

Like the
YOT
in the
POT.

But
that
YOTTLE
in
the
BOTTLE!

Some are friendly.
Some are NOT.

I like the
ZABLE
on the
TABLE.

And the
GHAIR under the CHAIR.

But that BOFA
    on the SOFA . . .

Well,
I wish
he wasn't there.

All those NUPBOARDS
in the CUPBOARDS.

They're good fun
to have about.

But that
NOOTH GRUSH
on my
TOOTH BRUSH . . .

Him
I could
do without!

The only one
I'm really scared of
is   that   VUG
under the RUG.

And that QUIMNEY
up the CHIMNEY . . .

I don't like him.
Not at all.

And it makes me sort of nervous
when the ZALL scoots down the HALL.

But the YEPS
on the STEPS —

They're great fun
to have around.

And so are
many, many
other friends
that I have found. . . .

. . . Like the TELLAR
and the NELLAR
and the GELLAR
and the DELLAR
and the BELLAR
and the WELLAR
and the ZELLAR
in the CELLAR.

. . . And the GEELING
on the CEILING . . .

. . . and
the
ZOWER
in
my
SHOWER . . .

. . . and the ZILLOW
   on my PILLOW.

   I don't care
   if you believe it.
   That's the kind of house
   I live in.
   And I hope
   we never leave it.

MR. BROWN CAN MOO! CAN YOU?

By
Dr. Seuss

MR. BROWN CAN MOO! CAN YOU?

By

Dr. Seuss

KLOPP KLOPP

KLOPP

HarperCollins *Children's Books*

™ & © Dr. Seuss Enterprises, L.P.
All Rights Reserved

3 5 7 9 10 8 6 4

ISBN 978-0-00-824000-4

© 1970 by Dr. Seuss Enterprises, L.P.,
renewed 1998 by Audrey S. Geisel
All Rights Reserved
Published by arrangement with Random House Inc.,
New York, USA
First published in the UK 1963
This edition published in the UK 2017 by
HarperColins *Children's Books,*
a division of HarperColins*Publishers* Ltd
1 London Bridge Street
London SE1 9GF

www.harpercollins.co.uk

Printed and bound in India by Replika Press Pvt. Ltd.

Oh, the wonderful things
Mr. Brown can do!
He can go like a cow.
He can go MOO MOO
Mr. Brown can do it.
How about you?

He can go like a bee.

Mr. Brown can

BUZZ

How about you?
Can you go

He can go like horse feet

He can go

EEK
EEK

like a squeaky shoe.

He can go
like a rooster . . .

COCK A
DOODLE
DOO

He can go
like an owl . . .

HOO HOO

HOO HOO

EEK EEK
EEK EEK
COCK-A-DOODLE-DOO
HOO HOO HOO HOO

How about you?

He can go like a train

CHOO CHOO
CHOO
CHOO
CHOO

Oh, the wonderful things
Mr. Brown can do!

MOO MOO
BUZZ BUZZ
POP POP POP
EEK EEK
HOO HOO
KLOPP KLOPP KLOPP
DIBBLE DIBBLE
DOPP DOPP
COCK-A-DOODLE-DOO

Mr. Brown can do it.
How about you?

. . . like the soft,
soft whisper
of a butterfly.

Maybe YOU can, too.
I think you ought to try.

He can go
like a horn. . .

. . . like a big cat drinking

He can go like a clock.
He can

Oh, the wonderful things
Mr. Brown can do!

BLURP BLURP
SLURP SLURP

COCK-A-DOODLE-DOO

KNOCK KNOCK KNOCK

and Hoo Hoo Hoo

He can even

SIZZLE
SIZZLE

He can do that, too,
like an egg
in a frying pan.
How about you?

Mr. Brown is smart,
as smart as they come!
He can do
a hippopotamus
chewing gum!

GRUM
GRUM
GRUM
GRUM
GRUM
GRUM
GRUM

Mr. Brown is
so smart
he can even do this:
he can even
make a noise
like a goldfish kiss!

BOOM BOOM BOOM

Mr. Brown is a wonder!

BOOM BOOM BOOM

Mr. Brown makes thunder!

He makes lightning!

SPLATT SPLATT SPLATT

And it's very, very hard
to make a noise like that.

Oh, the wonderful things
Mr. Brown can do!

Moo Moo
Buzz Buzz
Pop Pop Pop

Eek Eek
Hoo Hoo
Klopp Klopp Klopp

Dibble Dibble
Dopp Dopp
Cock-a-Doodle-Doo

Grum Grum
Grum Grum
Choo Choo Choo

Boom Boom
Splatt Splatt
Tick Tick Tock

Sizzle Sizzle
Blurp Blurp
Knock Knock Knock

A Slurp and a Whisper
and a Fish Kiss, too.

Mr. Brown can do it.
How about YOU?

GREEN EGGS
AND HAM

By
Dr. Seuss

HarperCollins *Children's Books*

3

4

5

7

That Sam-I-am!
That Sam-I-am!
I do not like
that Sam-I-am!

Do you like

green eggs and ham?

11

I do not like them,

Sam-I-am.

I do not like

green eggs and ham.

13

Would you like them

here or there?

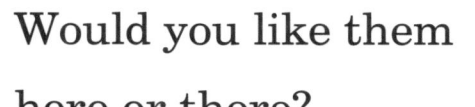

15

I would not like them
here or there.
I would not like them
anywhere.
I do not like
green eggs and ham.
I do not like them,
Sam-I-am.

16

17

Would you like them
in a house?
Would you like them
with a mouse?

I do not like them
in a house.
I do not like them
with a mouse.
I do not like them
here or there.
I do not like them
anywhere.
I do not like green eggs and ham.
I do not like them, Sam-I-am.

Would you eat them
in a box?
Would you eat them
with a fox?

Not in a box.

Not with a fox.

Not in a house.

Not with a mouse.

I would not eat them here or there.

I would not eat them anywhere.

I would not eat green eggs and ham.

I do not like them, Sam-I-am.

Would you? Could you?

In a car?

Eat them! Eat them!

Here they are.

I would not,
could not,
in a car.

You may like them.
You will see.
You may like them
in a tree!

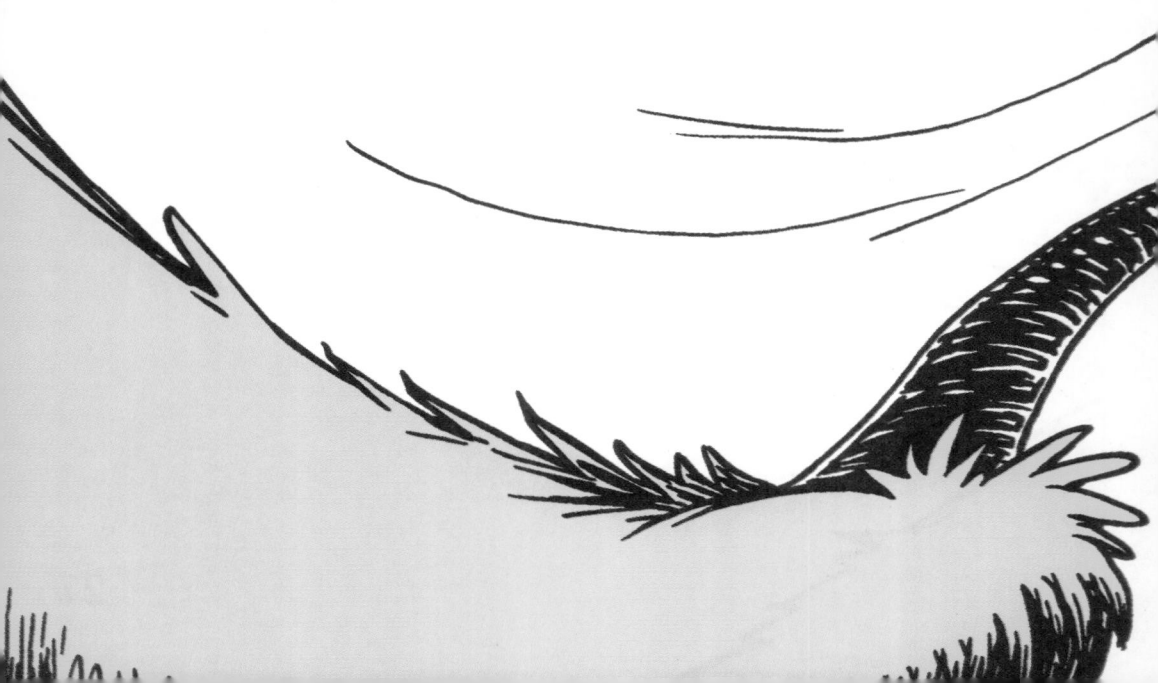

29

I would not, could not in a tree.
Not in a car!. You let me be.

I do not like them in a box.

I do not like them with a fox.

I do not like them in a house.

I do not like them with a mouse.

I do not like them here or there.

I do not like them anywhere.

I do not like green eggs and ham.

I do not like them, Sam-I-am.

A train! A train!
A train! A train!
Could you, would you,
on a train?

Not on a train! Not in a tree!

Not in a car! Sam! Let me be!

I would not, could not, in a box.

I could not, would not, with a fox.

I will not eat them with a mouse.

I will not eat them in a house.

I will not eat them here or there.

I will not eat them anywhere.

I do not eat green eggs and ham.

I do not like them, Sam-I-am.

Say!

In the dark?

Here in the dark!

Would you, could you, in the dark?

36

I would not, could not,
in the dark.

Would you, could you,

in the rain?

I would not, could not, in the rain.

Not in the dark. Not on a train.

Not in a car. Not in a tree.

I do not like them, Sam, you see.

Not in a house. Not in a box.

Not with a mouse. Not with a fox.

I will not eat them here or there.

I do not like them anywhere!

You do not like

green eggs and ham?

I do not
like them,
Sam-I-am.

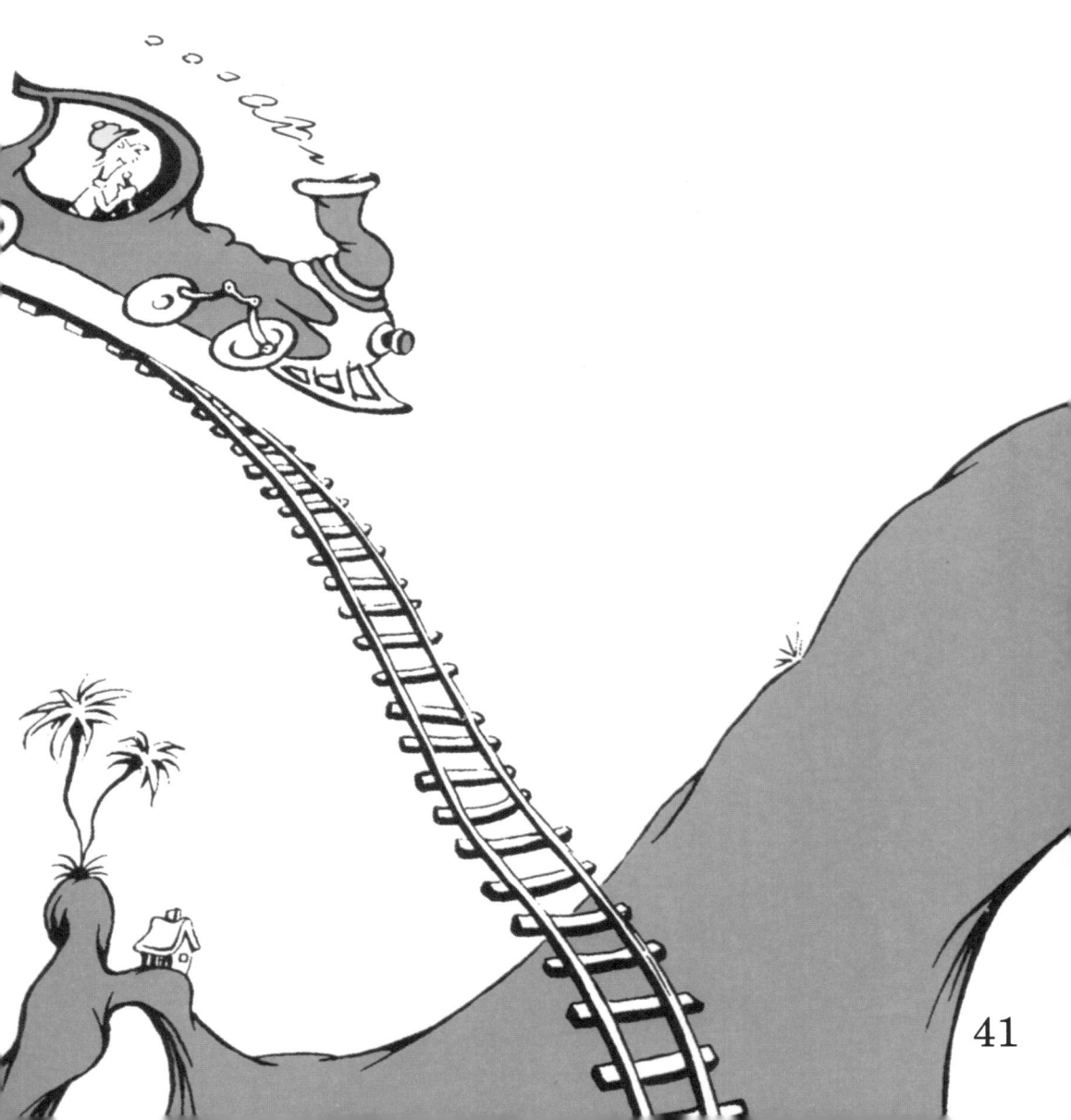

Could you, would you,
with a goat?

42

I would not,
could not,
with a goat!

Would you, could you,
on a boat?

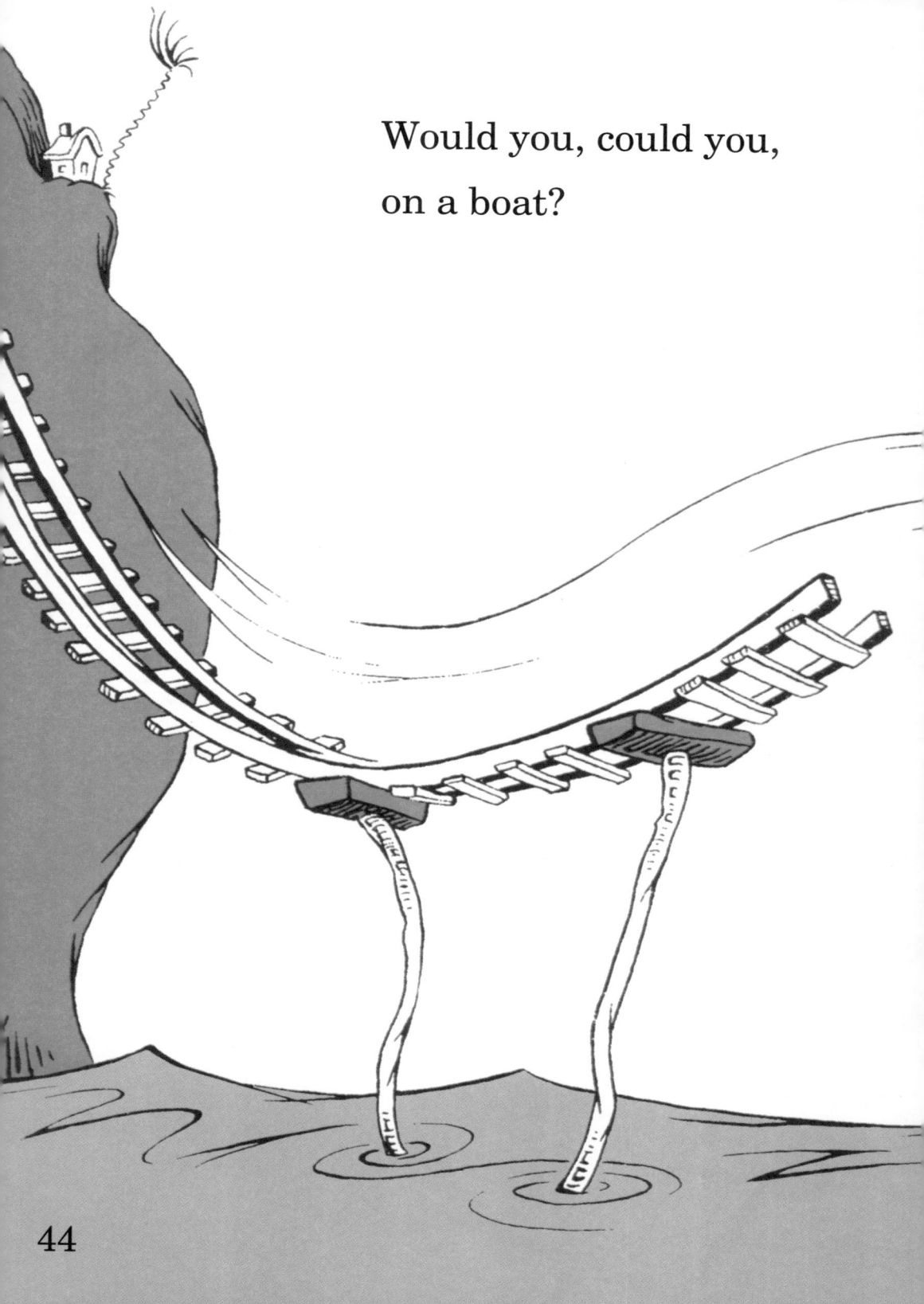

44

45

I could not, would not, on a boat.

I will not, will not, with a goat.

I will not eat them in the rain.

I will not eat them on a train.

Not in the dark! Not in a tree!

Not in a car! You let me be!

I do not like them in a box.

I do not like them with a fox.

I will not eat them in a house.

I do not like them with a mouse.

I do not like them here or there.

I do not like them ANYWHERE!

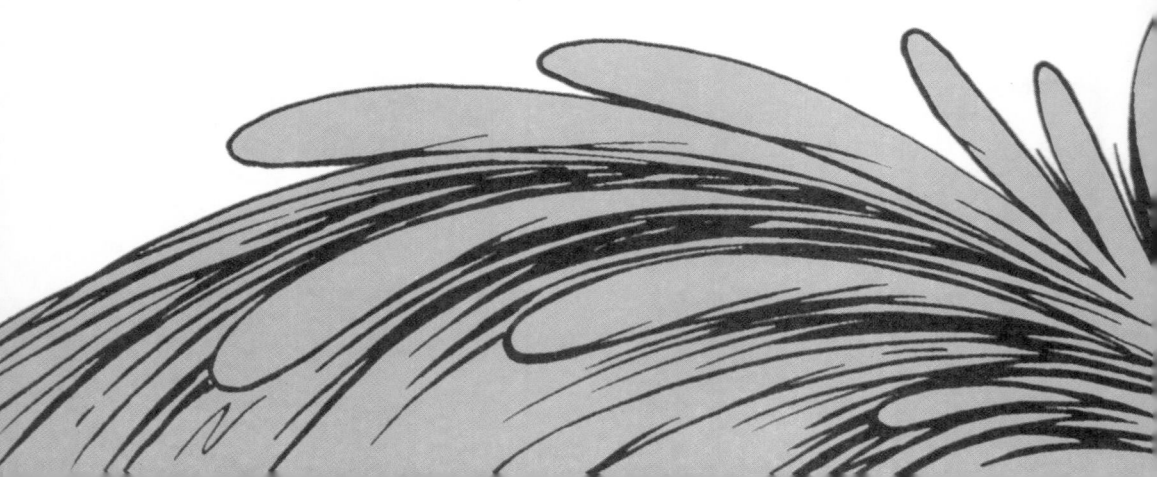

47

I do not like
green eggs
and ham!

I do not like them,
Sam-I-am.

51

You do not like them.
So you say.
Try them! Try them!
And you may.
Try them and you may, I say.

Sam!

If you will let me be,

I will try them.

You will see.

55

Sam!

I like green eggs and ham!

I do! I like them, Sam-I-am!

And I would eat them in a boat.

And I would eat them with a goat . . .

And I will eat them in the rain.

And in the dark. And on a train.

And in a car. And in a tree.

They are so good, so good, you see!

So I will eat them in a box.

And I will eat them with a fox.

And I will eat them in a house.

And I will eat them with a mouse.

And I will eat them here and there.

I will eat them ANYWHERE!

I do so like
green eggs and ham!
Thank you!
Thank you,
Sam-I-am!

THE LORAX

By

Dr. Seuss

HarperCollins *Children's Books*

For AUDREY, LARK *and* LEA
With Love

The Cat in the Hat
™ & © Dr. Seuss Enterprises, L.P. 1957
All Rights Reserved

A CIP catalogue record for this title is available from
the British Library.
No part of this publication may be reproduced, stored
in a retrieval system or transmitted in any form or by
any means, electronic, mechanical, photocopying,
recording or otherwise, without the prior permission of
HarperCollins Publishers Ltd, 1 London Bridge Street
London SE1 9GF

3 5 7 9 10 8 6 4

ISBN 978-0-00-820392-4

The Lorax
© 1971, 1999 by Dr. Seuss Enterprises, L.P.
All Rights Reserved
Published by arrangement with Random House Inc.,
New York, USA
First published in the UK 1972
This edition published in the UK 2004 revised by
HarperCollins *Children's Books* 2017, a division of
HaperCollins*Publishers* Ltd, 1 London Bridge Street
London SE1 9GF

Visit our website at:
www.harpercollins.co.uk

Printed and bound in India by Replika Press Pvt. Ltd.

At the far end of town
where the Grickle-grass grows
and the wind smells slow-and-sour when it blows
and no birds ever sing excepting old crows . . .
is the Street of the Lifted Lorax.

And deep in the Grickle-grass, some people say,
if you look deep enough you can still see, today,
where the Lorax once stood
just as long as it could
before somebody lifted the Lorax away.

What *was* the Lorax?
And why was it there?
And why was it lifted and taken somewhere
from the far end of town where the Grickle-grass grows?
The old Once-ler still lives here.
Ask him. *He* knows.

You won't see the Once-ler.
Don't knock at his door.
He stays in his Lerkim on top of his store.
He lurks in his Lerkim, cold under the roof,
where he makes his own clothes
out of miff-muffered moof.
And on special dank midnights in August,
he peeks
out of the shutters
and sometimes he speaks
and tells how the Lorax was lifted away.

He'll tell you, perhaps . . .
if you're willing to pay.

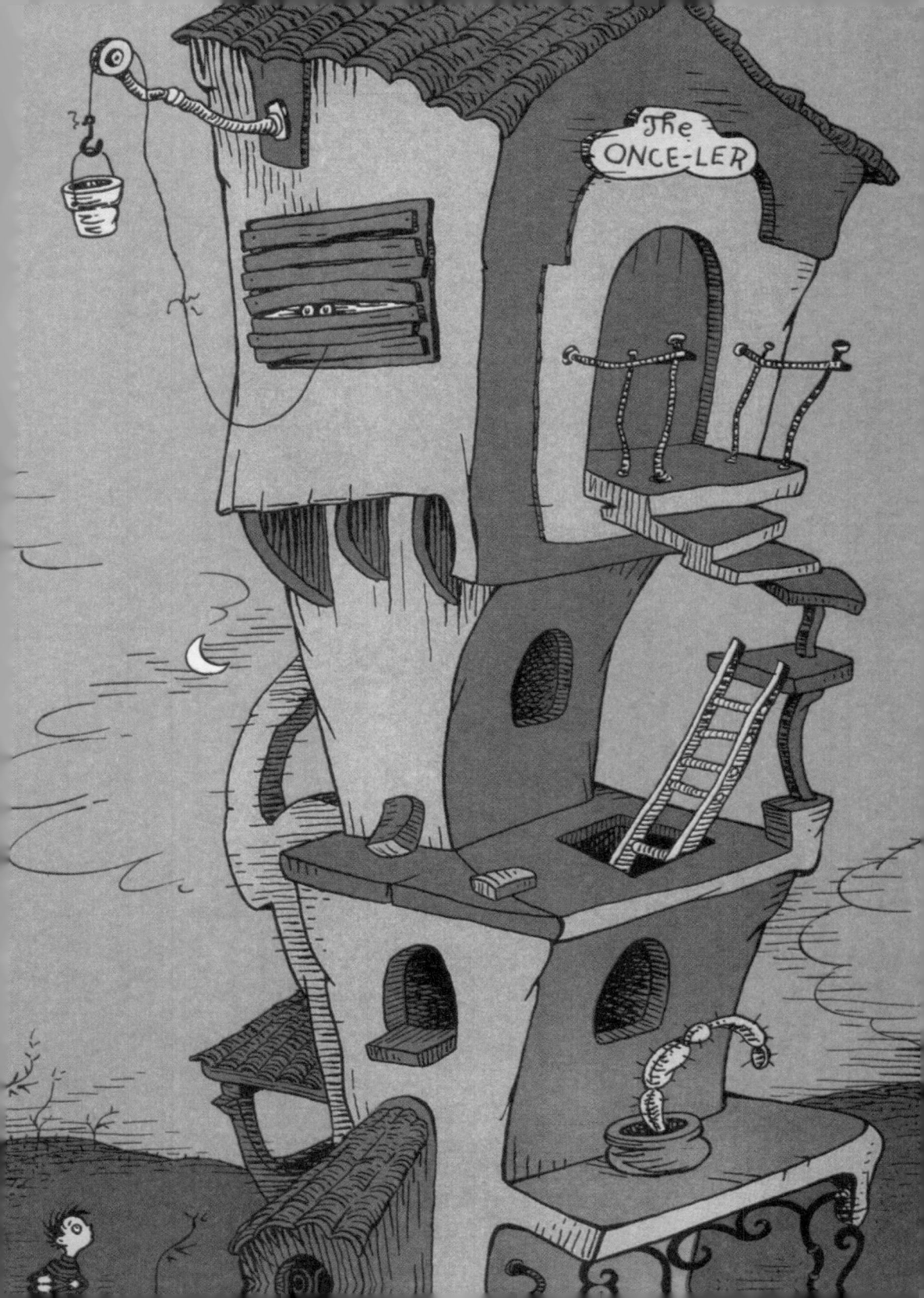

On the end of a rope
he lets down a tin pail
and you have to toss in fifteen pence
and a nail
and the shell of a great-great-great-
grandfather snail.

Then he pulls up the pail,
makes a most careful count
to see if you've paid him
the proper amount.

Then he hides what you paid him
away in his Snuvv,
his secret strange hole
in his gruvvulous glove.

Then he grunts, "I will call you by Whisper-ma-Phone,
for the secrets I tell are for your ears alone."

SLUPP!
Down slupps the Whisper-ma-Phone to your ear
and the old Once-ler's whispers are not very clear,
since they have to come down
through a snergelly hose,
and he sounds
as if he had
smallish bees up his nose.

"Now I'll tell you," he says, with his teeth sounding grey
"how the Lorax got lifted and taken away . . .

It all started way back . . .
such a long, long time back . . .

Way back in the days when the grass was still green
and the pond was still wet
and the clouds were still clean,
and the song of the Swomee-Swans rang out in space . . .
one morning, I came to this glorious place.
And I first saw the trees!
The Truffula Trees!
The bright-coloured tufts of the Truffula Trees!
Mile after mile in the fresh morning breeze.

ONCE-LER
WAGON

And, under the trees, I saw Brown Bar-ba-loots
frisking about in their Bar-ba-loot suits
as they played in the shade and ate Truffula Fruits.

From the rippulous pond
came the comfortable sound
of the Humming-Fish humming
while splashing around.

But those *trees!* Those *trees!*
Those Truffula Trees!
All my life I'd been searching
for trees such as these.
The touch of their tufts
was much softer than silk.
And they had the sweet smell
of fresh butterfly milk.

I felt a great leaping
of joy in my heart.
I knew just what I'd do!
I unloaded my cart.

In no time at all, I had built a small shop.
Then I chopped down a Truffula Tree with one chop.
And with great skilful skill and with great speedy speed,
I took the soft tuft. And I knitted a Thneed!

The instant I'd finished, I heard a *ga-Zump!*
I looked.
I saw something pop out of the stump
of the tree I'd chopped down. It was sort of a man.
Describe him? ...That's hard. I don't know if I can.

He was shortish. And oldish.
And brownish. And mossy.
And he spoke with a voice
that was sharpish and bossy.

"Mister!" he said with a sawdusty sneeze,
"I am the Lorax. I speak for the trees.
I speak for the trees, for the trees have no tongues.
And I'm asking you, sir, at the top of my lungs"–
he was very upset as he shouted and puffed–
"What's that THING you've made out of my Truffula tuft?"

"Look, Lorax," I said. "There's no cause for alarm.
I chopped just one tree. I am doing no harm.
I'm being quite useful. This thing is a Thneed.
A Thneed's a Fine-Something-That-All-People-Need!
It's a shirt. It's a sock. It's a glove. It's a hat.
But it has *other* uses. Yes, far beyond that.
You can use it for carpets. For pillows! For sheets!
Or curtains! Or covers for bicycle seats!"

The Lorax siad,
"Sir! You are crazy with greed.
There is no one on earth
who would buy that fool Thneed!"

But the very next minute I proved he was wrong.
For, just at that minute, a chap came along,
and he thought that the Thneed I had knitted was great.
He happily bought it for three ninety-eight.

I laughed at the Lorax, "You poor stupid guy!
You never can tell what some people will buy."

"I repeat," cried the Lorax,
"I speak for the trees!"

"I'm busy," I told him.
"Shut up, if you please."

I rushed 'cross the room, and in no time at all,
built a radio-phone. I put in a quick call.
I called all my brothers and uncles and aunts
and I said, "Listen here! Here's a wonderful chance
for the whole Once-ler Family to get mighty rich!
Get over here fast! Take the road to North Nitch.
Turn left at Weehawken. Sharp right at South Stitch."

And, in no time at all,
in the factory I built,
the whole Once-ler Family
was working full tilt.
We were all knitting Thneeds
just as busy as bees,
to the sound of the chopping
of Truffula Trees.

Then . . .
Oh! Baby! Oh!
How my business did grow!
Now, chopping one tree
at a time
was too slow.

So I quickly invented my Super-Axe-Hacker
which whacked off four Truffula Trees at one smacker.
We were making Thneeds
four times as fast as before!
And that Lorax? . . .
He didn't show up any more.

But the next week
he knocked
on my new office door.

He snapped, "I'm the Lorax who speaks for the trees
which you seem to be chopping as fast as you please.
But I'm *also* in charge of the Brown Bar-ba-loots
who played in the shade in their Bar-ba-loot suits
and happily lived, eating Truffula Fruits.

"NOW . . .thanks to your hacking my trees to the ground,
there's not enough Truffula Fruit to go 'round.
And my poor Bar-ba-loots are all getting the crummies
because they have gas, and no food, in their tummies!

"They loved living here. But I can't let them stay.
They'll have to find food. And I hope that they may.
Good luck, boys," he cried. And he sent them away.

I, the Once-ler, felt sad
as I watched them all go.
BUT. . .
business is business!
And business must grow
regardless of crummies in tummies, you know.

I meant no harm. I most truly did not.
But I had to grow bigger. So bigger I got.
I biggered my factory. I biggered my roads.
I biggered my wagons. I biggered the loads
of the Thneeds I shipped out. I was shipping them forth
to the South! To the East! To the West! To the North!
I went right on biggering . . . selling more Thneeds.
And I biggered my money, which everyone needs.

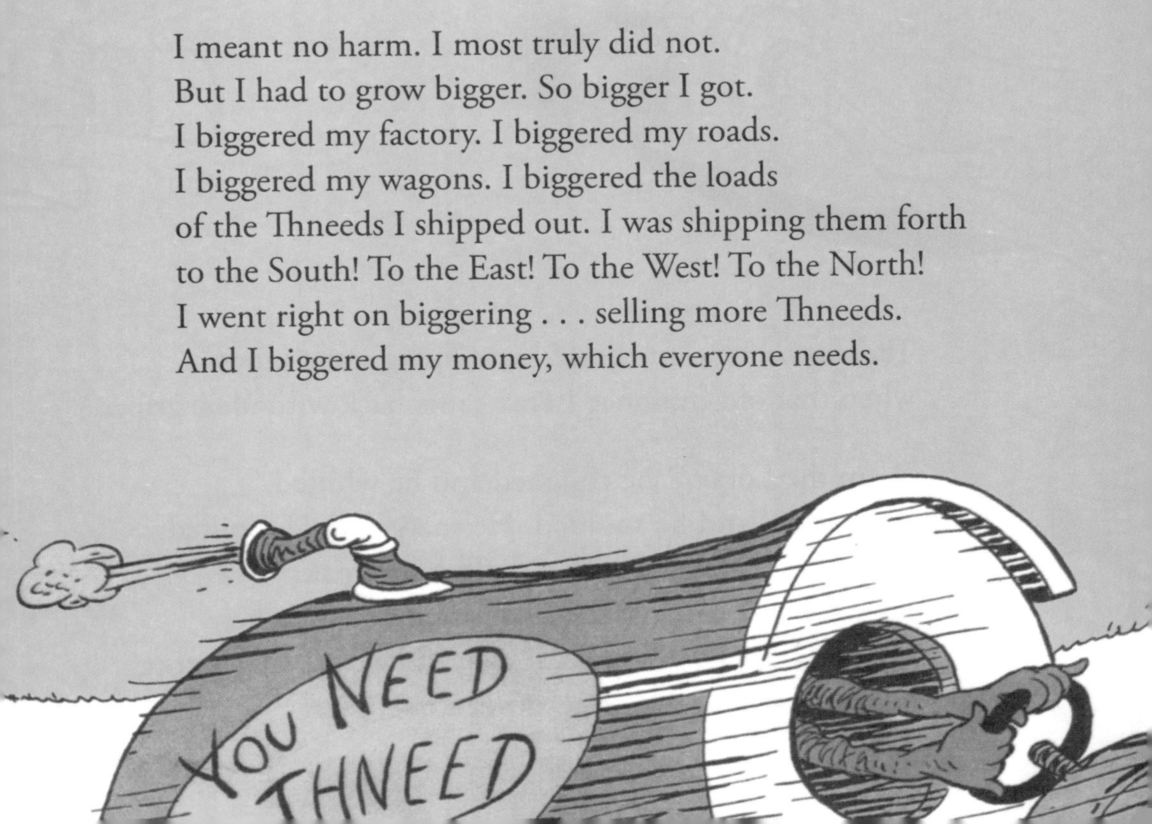

YOU NEED
THNEED

Then *again* he came back! I was fixing some pipes
when that old-nuisance Lorax came back with *more* gripes.

"I am the Lorax," he coughed and he whiffed.
He sneezed and he snuffled. He snarggled. He sniffed.
"Once-ler!" he cried with a cruffulous croak.
"Once-ler! You're making such smogulous smoke!
My poor Swomee-Swans . . . why, they can't sing a note!
No one can sing who has smog in his throat.

"And so," said the Lorax,
"–please pardon my cough–
they cannot live here.
So I'm sending them off.

"Where will they go? . . .
I don't hopefully know.

They may have to fly for a month . . . or a year . . .
To escape from the smog you've smogged-up around here.

"What's *more*," snapped the Lorax. (His dander was up.)
"Let me say a few words about Gluppity-Glupp.
Your machinery chugs on, day and night without stop
making Gluppity-Glupp. Also Schloppity-Schlopp.
And what do you do with this leftover goo? . . .
I'll show you. You dirty old Once-ler man, you!

"You're glumping the pond where the Humming-Fish hummed!
No more can they hum, for their gills are all gummed.
So I'm sending them off. Oh, their future is dreary.
They'll walk on their fins and get woefully weary
in search of some water that isn't so smeary.
I hear things are just as bad up in Lake Erie."

And then I got mad.
I got terribly mad.
I yelled at the Lorax, "Now listen here, Dad!
All you do is yap-yap and say, 'Bad! Bad! Bad! Bad!'
Well, I have my rights, sir, and I'm telling *you*
I intend to go on doing just what I do!
And, for your information, you Lorax, I'm figgering
on biggering

    and BIGGERING

        and BIGGERING

           and BIGGERING,

turning MORE Truffula Trees into Thneeds
which everyone, EVERYONE, *EVERYONE* needs!"

And at that very moment, we heard a loud whack!
From outside in the fields came a sickening smack
of an axe on a tree. Then we heard the tree fall.
The very last Truffula Tree of them all!

THNEEDS

YOU NEED A THNEED

No more trees. No more Thneeds. No more work to be done.
So, in no time, my uncles and aunts, every one,
all waved me good-bye. They jumped into my cars
and drove away under the smoke-smuggered stars.

Now all that was left 'neath the bad-smelling sky
was my big empty factory. . .
the Lorax. . .
and I.

The Lorax said nothing. Just gave me a glance . . .
just gave me a very sad, sad backward glance . . .
as he lifted himself by the seat of his pants.
And I'll never forget the grim look on his face
when he heisted himself and took leave of this place,
through a hole in the smog, without leaving a trace.

And all that the Lorax left here in this mess
was a small pile of rocks, with the one word . . .
"UNLESS."
Whatever *that* meant, well, I just couldn't guess.

That was long, long ago.
But each day since that day
I've sat here and worried
and worried away.
Through the years, while my buildings
have fallen apart,
I've worried about it
with all of my heart.

"But *now*," says the Once ler,.
"Now that *you're* here,
the word of the Lorax seems perfectly clear.
UNLESS someone like you
cares a whole awful lot,
nothing is going to get better.
It's not.

"SO. . .
Catch!" calls the Once-ler.
He lets something fall.
"It's a Truffula Seed.
It's the last one of all!
You're in charge of the last of the Truffula Seeds.
And Truffula Trees are what everyone needs.
Plant a new Truffula. Treat it with care.
Give it clean water. And feed it fresh air.
Grow a forest. Protect it from axes that hack.
Then the Lorax
and all of his friends
may come back."

HORTON HEARS
A WHO!

By

Dr. Seuss

HarperCollins *Children's Books*

™ & © Dr. Seuss Enterprises, L.P.
All Rights Reserved

A CIP catalogue record for this title is available from the
British Library.
No part of this publication may be reproduced, stored
in a retrieval system or transmitted in any form or by
any means, electronic, mechanical, photocopying,
recording or otherwise, without the prior permission of
HarperCollins Publishers Ltd, 1 London Bridge Street
London SE1 9GF

3 5 7 9 10 8 6 4

ISBN 978-0-00-824002-8

Copyright © 1954, 1982, by Dr. Seuss Enterprises, L.P.
All Rights Reserved

Published by arrangement with Random House Inc.,
New York, USA
First published in the UK in 1976
This edition published in the UK in 2017 by
HarperCollins *Children's Books,*
a division of HarperCollins*Publishers* Ltd
1 London Bridge Street
London SE1 9GF.

www.harpercollins.co.uk

Printed and bound in India by Replika Press Pvt. Ltd.

For My Great Friend,
Mitsugi Nakamura
of Kyoto,
Japan.

On the fifteenth of May, in the Jungle of Nool,
In the heat of the day, in the cool of the pool,
He was splashing . . . enjoying the jungle's great joys . . .
When Horton the elephant heard a small noise.

So Horton stopped splashing. He looked towards the sound.
"That's funny," thought Horton. "There's no one around."
Then he heard it again! Just a very faint yelp
As if some tiny person were calling for help.
"I'll help you," said Horton. "But *who* are you? *Where?*"
He looked and he looked. He could see nothing there
But a small speck of dust blowing past through the air.

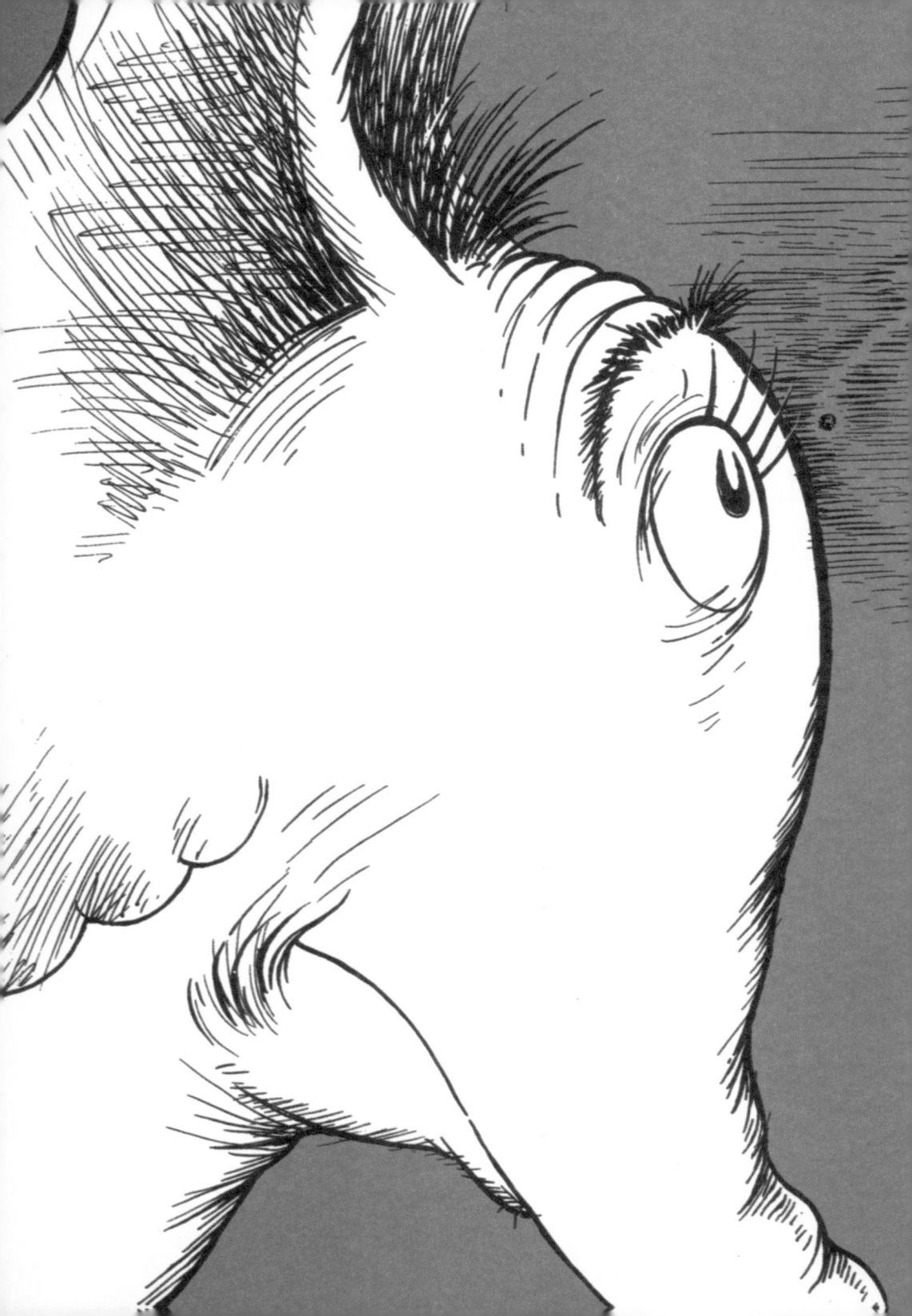

"I say!" murmured Horton. "I've never heard tell
Of a small speck of dust that is able to yell.
So you know what I think? . . . Why, I think that there must
Be someone on top of that small speck of dust!
Some sort of a creature of *very* small size,
Too small to be seen by an elephant's eyes. . .

"...some poor little person who's shaking with fear
That he'll blow in the pool! He has no way to steer!
I'll just have to save him. Because, after all,
A person's a person, no matter how small."

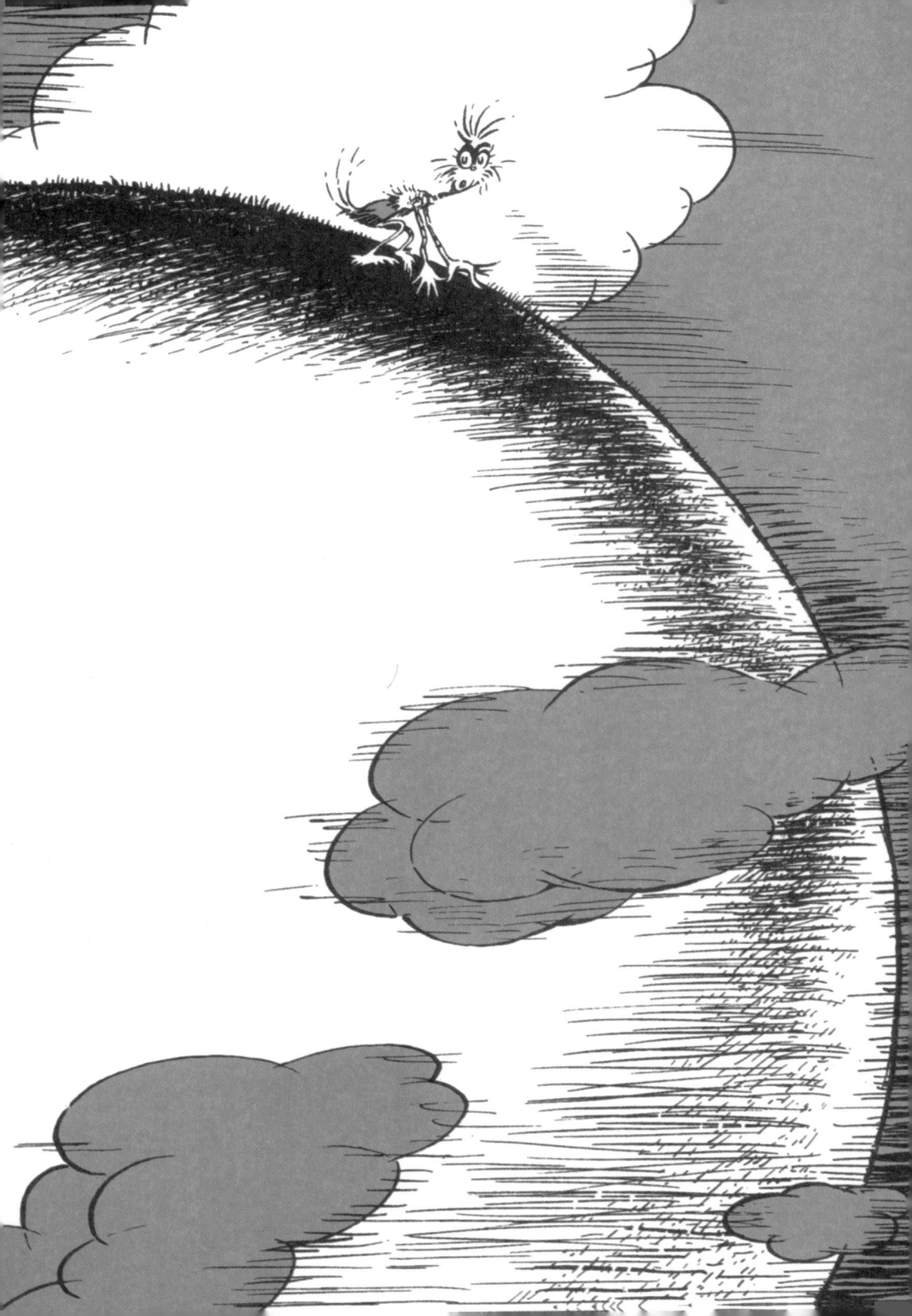

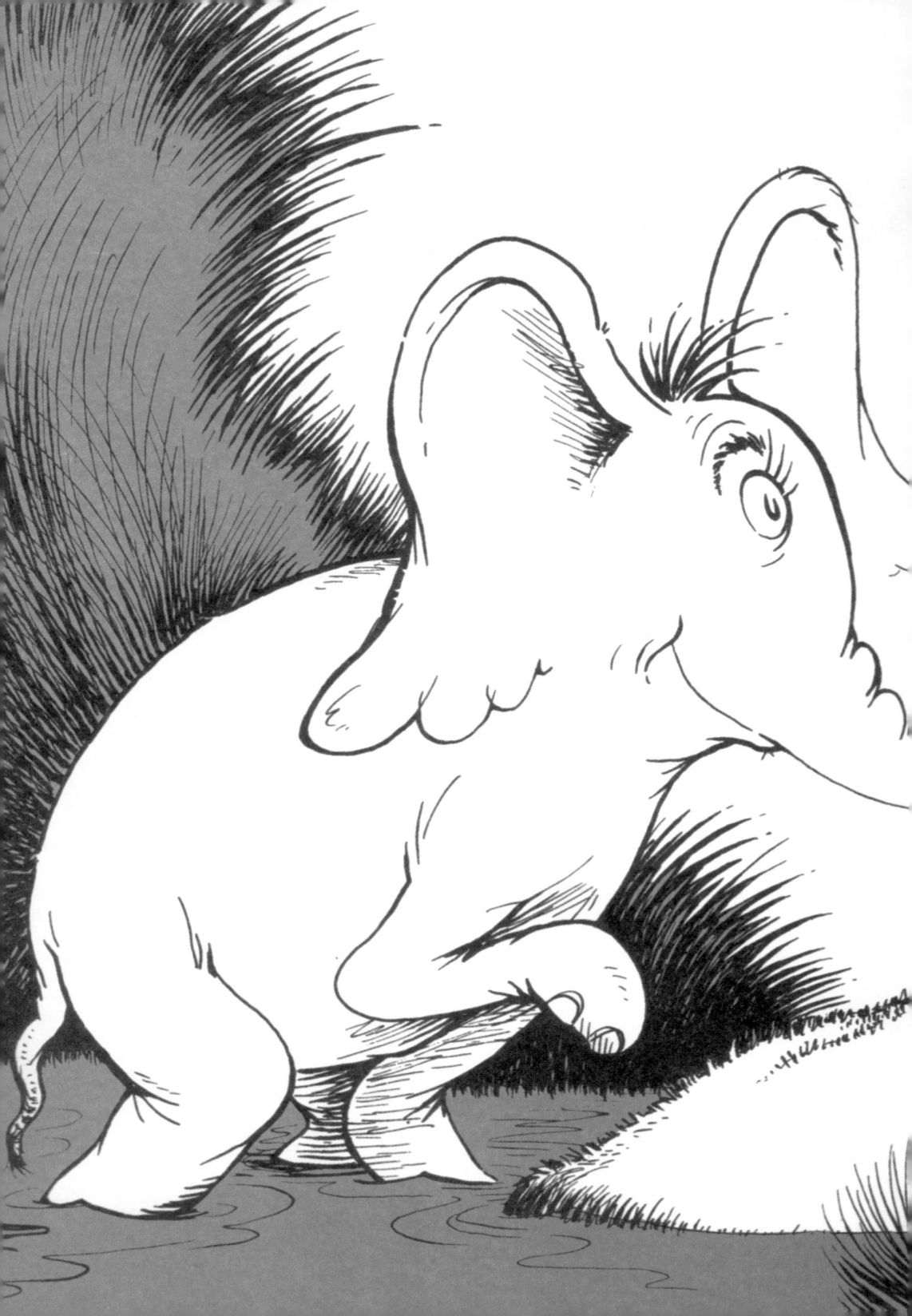

So, gently, and using the greatest of care,
The elephant stretched his great trunk through the air,
And he lifted the dust speck and carried it over
And placed it down, safe, on a very soft clover.

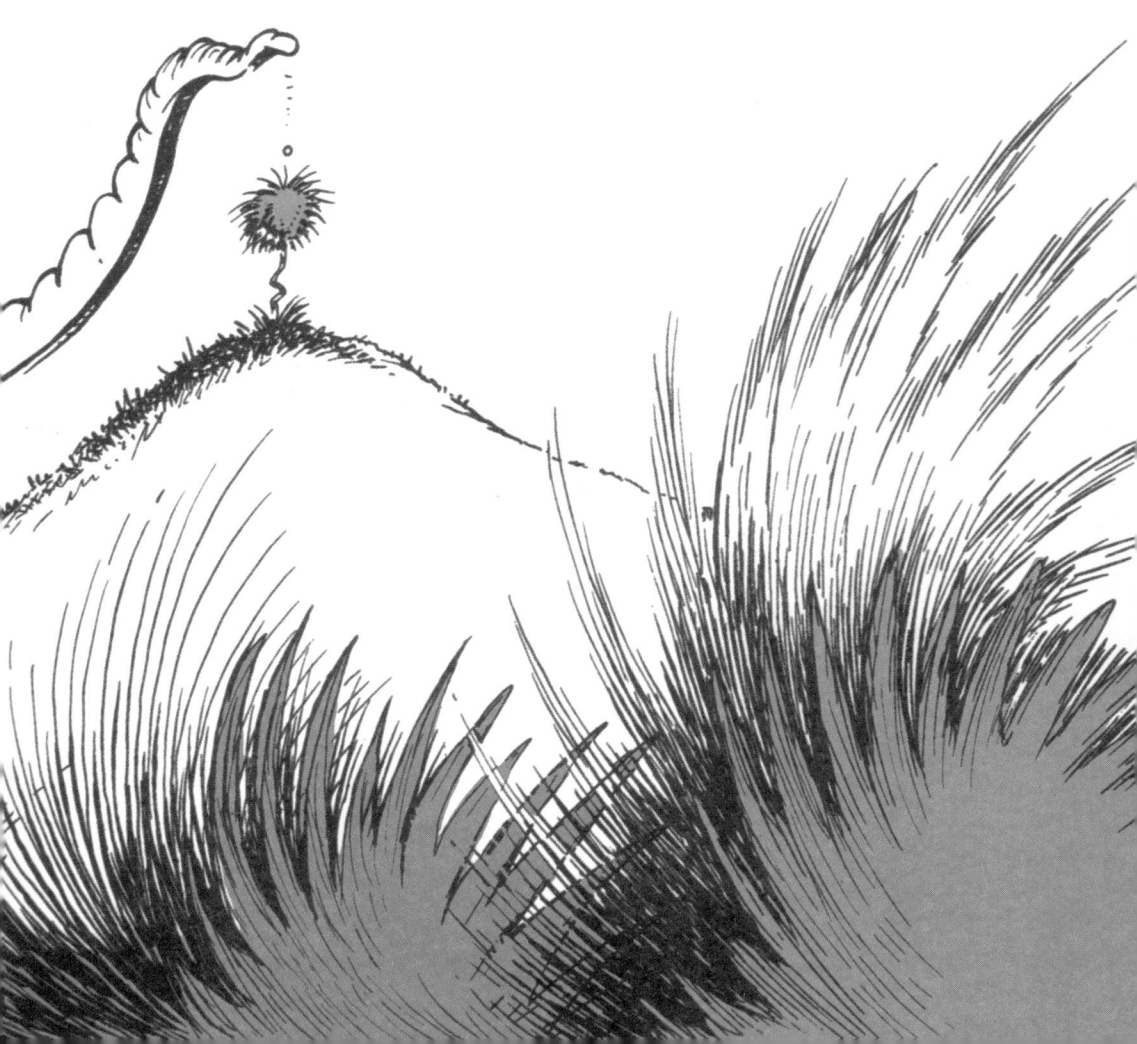

"Humpf!" humpfed a voice. 'Twas a sour kangaroo.
And the young kangaroo in her pouch said "Humpf!" too
"Why, that speck is as small as the head of a pin.
A person on *that?* . . . Why, there never has been!"

"Believe me," said Horton. "I tell you sincerely,
My ears are quite keen and I heard him quite clearly.
I *know* there's a person down there. And, what's more,
Quite likely there's two. Even three. Even four.
Quite likely . . .

". . . a family, for all that we know!
A family with children just starting to grow.
So, please," Horton said, "as a favour to me,
Try not to disturb them. Just please let them be."

"I think you're a fool!" laughed the sour kangaroo
And the young kangaroo in her pouch said, "Me, too!
You're the biggest blame fool in the Jungle of Nool!"
And the kangaroos plunged in the cool of the pool.
"What terrible splashing!" the elephant frowned.
"I can't let my very small persons get drowned!
I've *got* to protect them. I'm bigger than they."
So he plucked up the clover and hustled away.

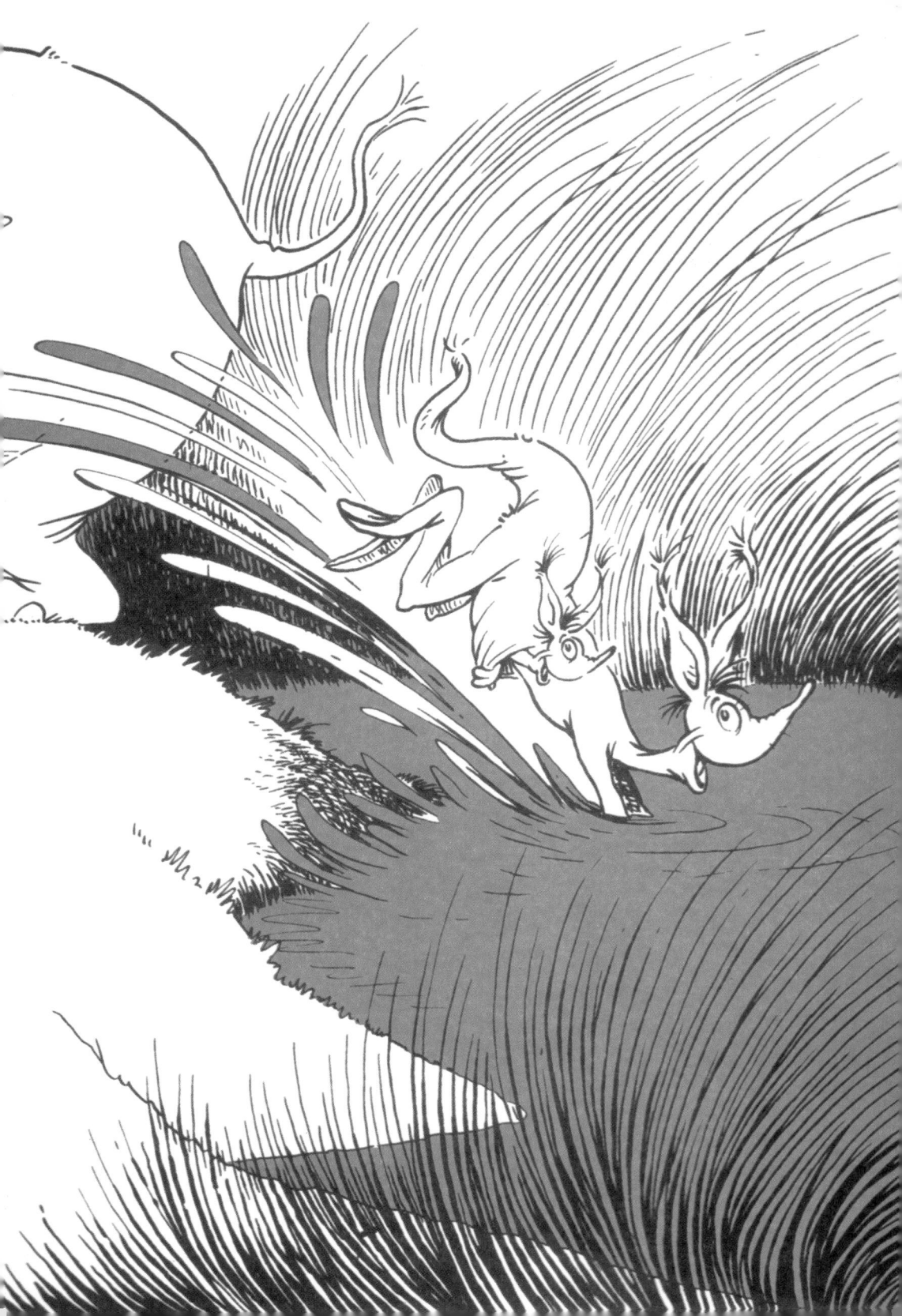

Through the high jungle tree tops, the news quickly spread:
"He talks to a dust speck! He's out of his head!
Just look at him walk with that speck on that flower!"
And Horton walked, worrying, almost an hour.
"Should I put this speck down? . . ." Horton thought with alarm.
"If I do, these small persons may come to great harm.
I *can't* put it down. And I *won't*! After all
A person's a person. No matter how small.

Then Horton stopped walking.
The speck-voice was talking!
The voice was so faint he could just barely hear it.
"Speak *up,* please," said Horton. He put his ear near it.
"My friend," came the voice, "you're a *very* fine friend.
You've helped all us folks on this dust speck no end.
You've saved all our houses, our ceilings and floors.
You've saved all our churches and grocery stores."

"You mean . . ." Horton gasped, "you have *buildings* there, *too?*"

"Oh, yes," piped the voice. "We most certainly do. . . .
"I know," called the voice, "I'm too small to be seen
But I'm Mayor of a town that is friendly and clean.
Our buildings, to you, would seem terribly small
But to us, who aren't big, they are wonderfully tall.
My town is called *Who*-ville, for I am a *Who*
And we *Whos* are all thankful and grateful to you."

And Horton called back to the Mayor of the town,
"You're safe now. Don't worry. I won't let you down."

But, just as he spoke to the Mayor of the speck,
Three big jungle monkeys climbed up Horton's neck!
The Wickersham Brothers came shouting, "What rot!
This elephant's talking to *Whos* who are *not!*
There *aren't* any *Whos!* And they *don't* have a Mayor!
And *we're* going to stop all this nonsense! *So there!*"

They snatched Horton's clover! They carried it off
To a black-bottomed eagle named Vlad Vlad-i-koff,
A mighty strong eagle, of very swift wing,
And they said, "Will you kindly get rid of this thing?"
And, before the poor elephant even could speak,
That eagle flew off with the flower in his beak.

All that late afternoon and far into the night
That black-bottomed bird flapped his wings in fast flight,
While Horton chased after, with groans, over stones
That tattered his toenails and battered his bones,
And begged, "Please don't harm all my little folks, who
Have as much right to live as us bigger folks do!"

But far, far beyond him, that eagle kept flapping
And over his shoulder called back, "Quit your yapping.
I'll fly the night through. I'm a bird. I don't mind it.
And I'll hide this, tomorrow, where *you'll* never find it!"

And at 6.:56 the next morning he did it.
It sure was a terrible place that he hid it.
He let that small clover drop somewhere inside
Of a great patch of clovers a hundred miles wide!
"Find THAT!" sneered the bird. "But I think you will fail."
And he left
With a flip
Of his black-bottomed tail.

"I'll find it!" cried Horton. "I'll find it or bust!
I SHALL find my friends on my small speck of dust!"
And clover, by clover, by clover with care
He picked up and searched them, and called, "Are you there?"
But clover, by clover, by clover he found
That the one that he sought for was just not around.
And by noon poor old Horton, more dead than alive,
Had picked, searched, and piled up, nine thousand and five.

Then, on through the afternoon, hour after hour...
Till he found them at last! On the three millionth flower!
"My friends!" cried the elephant. "Tell me! Do tell!
Are you safe? Are you sound? Are you whole? Are you well.?"

From down on the speck came the voice of the Mayor:

"We've *really* had trouble! Much more than our share.
When that black-bottomed birdie let go and we dropped,
We landed so hard that our clocks have all stopped.
Our tea-pots are broken. Our rocking-chairs smashed.
And our bicycle tyres all blew up when we crashed.
So, Horton, *please!*" pleaded that voice of the Mayor's,
"Will you stick by us *Whos* while we're making repairs?"

"Of course," Horton answered. "Of course I will stick.
I'll stick by you small folks through thin and through thick

"Humpf!"
Humpfed a voice!
"For almost two days you've run wild and insisted
On chatting with persons who've never existed.
Such carryings-on in our peaceable jungle!
We've had quite enough of your bellowing bungle!
And I'm here to state," snapped the big kangaroo,
"That your silly nonsensical game is all through!"
And the young kangaroo in her pouch said, "Me, too!"

"With the help of the Wickersham Brothers and dozens
Of Wickersham Uncles and Wickersham Cousins
And Wickersham In-Laws, whose help I've engaged,
You're going to be roped! And you're going to be caged!
And, as for your dust speck...*hah! That* we shall boil
In a hot steaming kettle of Beezle-Nut oil!"

"*Boil* it?..." gasped Horton!
"Oh, that you *can't* do!
It's all full of persons!
They'll *prove* it to you!"

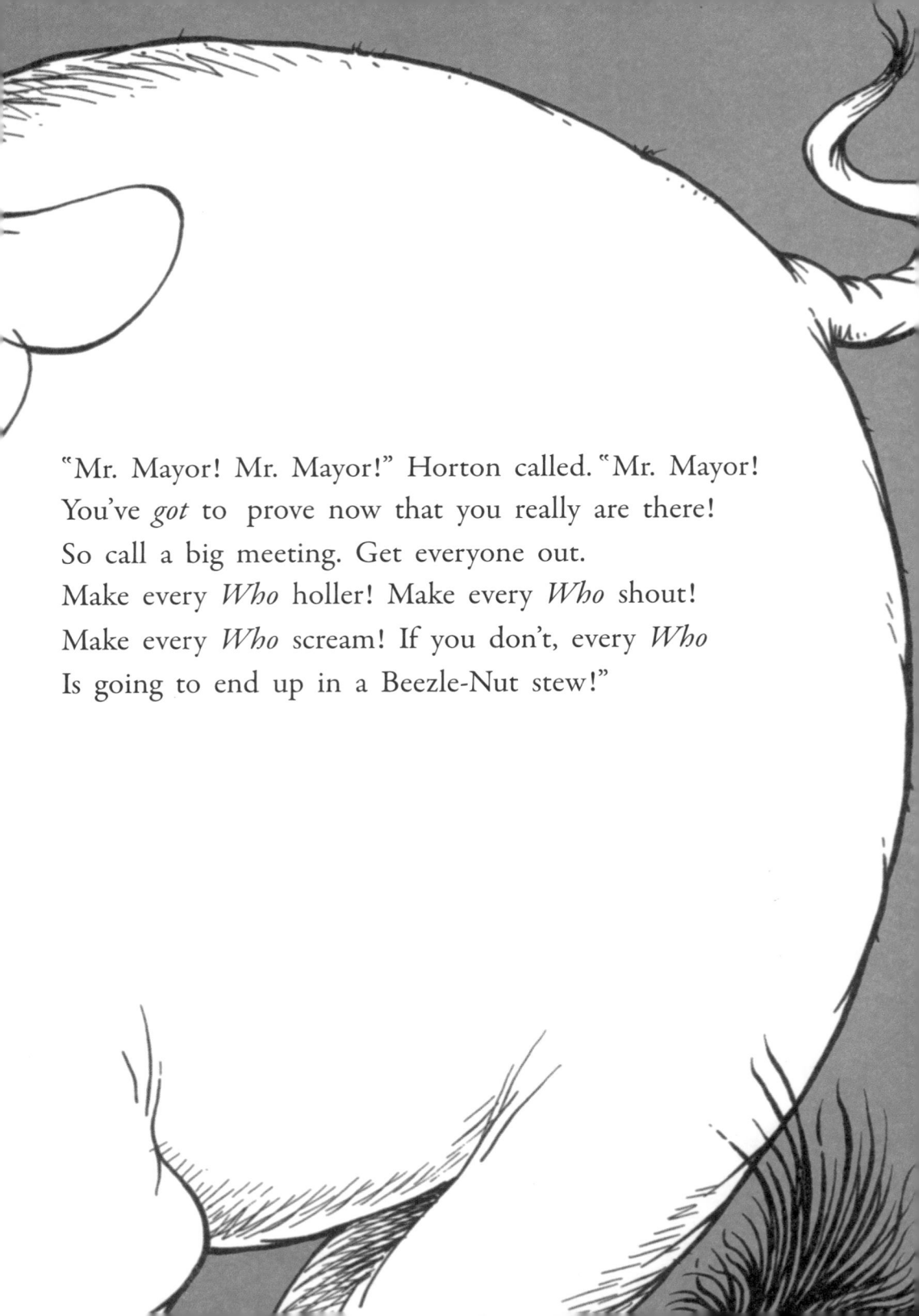

"Mr. Mayor! Mr. Mayor!" Horton called. "Mr. Mayor!
You've *got* to prove now that you really are there!
So call a big meeting. Get everyone out.
Make every *Who* holler! Make every *Who* shout!
Make every *Who* scream! If you don't, every *Who*
Is going to end up in a Beezle-Nut stew!"

And, down on the dust speck, the scared little Mayor
Quick called a big meeting in *Who*-ville Town Square.
And his people cried loudly. They cried out in fear:
We are here! We are here! We are here! We are here!"

The elephant smiled: "That was clear as a bell.
You kangaroos surely heard *that* very well."
"All I heard," snapped the big kangaroo "was the breeze,
And the faint sound of wind through the far-distant trees.
I heard no small voices. And you didn't either."
And the young kangaroo in her pouch said, "Me, neither."

"Grab him!" they shouted. "And cage the big dope!
Lasso his stomach with ten miles of rope!
Tie the knots tight so he'll *never* shake loose!
Then dunk that dumb speck in the Beezle-Nut juice!"

Horton fought back with great vigour and vim
But the Wickersham gang was too many for him.
They beat him! They mauled him! They started to haul
Him into his cage! But he managed to call
To the Mayor: 'Don't give up! I believe in you all!
A person's a person, no matter how small!
And you very small persons will *not* have to die
If you make yourselves heard! *So come on, now, and TRY!*"

The Mayor grabbed a tom-tom. He started to smack it.
And, all over *Who*-ville, they whooped up a racket.
They rattled tin kettles! They beat on brass pans,
On garbage pail tops and old cranberry cans!
They blew on bazookas and blasted great toots
On clarinets, oom-pahs and boom-pahs and flutes!

Great gusts of loud racket rang high through the air.
They rattled and shook the whole sky! And the Mayor
Called up through the howling mad hullabaloo:
"Hey, Horton! *How's this?* Is our sound coming through?"

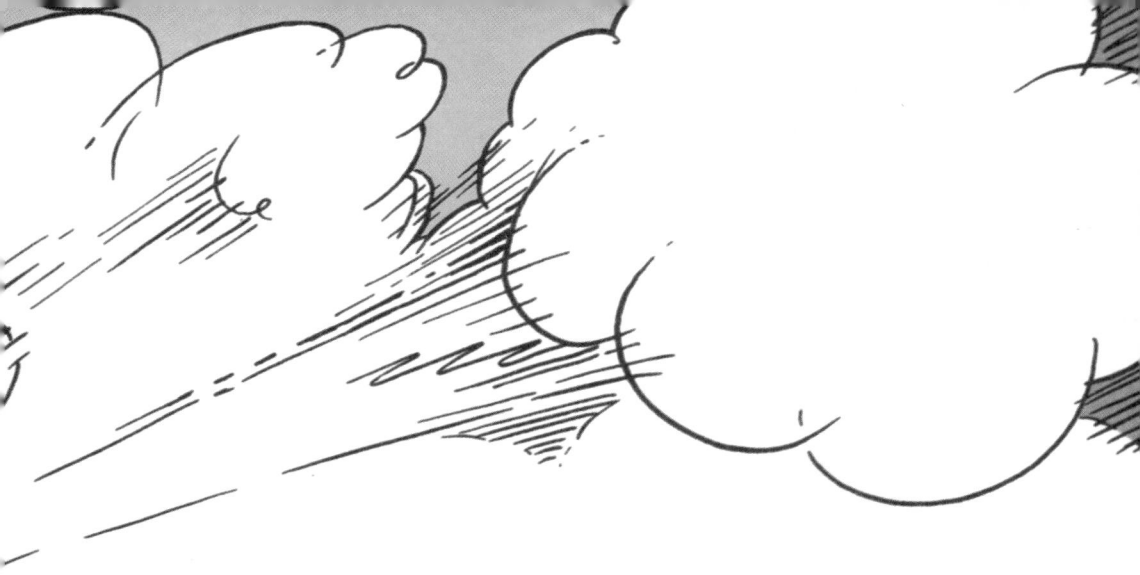

And Horton called back, "I can hear you just fine.
But the kangaroos' ears aren't as strong, quite, as mine.
They don't hear a thing! Are you *sure* all your boys
Are doing their best? Are they ALL making noise?
Are you sure every *Who* down in *Who*-ville is working?
Quick! Look through your town! Is there anyone shirking?"

Through the town rushed the Mayor, from the east to the west.
But *every*one seemed to be doing his best.
*Every*one seemed to be yapping or yipping!
*Every*one seemed to be beeping or bipping!
But it *wasn't enough*, all this ruckus and roar!
He HAD to find someone to help him make more.
He raced through each building! He searched floor-to-floor!

And, just as he felt he was getting nowhere,
And almost about to give up in despair,
He suddenly burst through a door and that Mayor
Discovered one shirker! Quite hidden away
In the Fairfax Apartments (Apartment 12-J)
A very small, *very* small shirker named Jo-Jo
Was standing, just standing, and bouncing a Yo-Yo!
Not making a sound! Not a yipp! Not a chirp!
And the Mayor rushed inside and he grabbed the young twerp!

And he climbed with the lad up the Eiffelberg Tower.

"This," cried the Mayor, "is your town's darkest hour!
The time for all *Whos* who have blood that is red
To come to the aid of their country!" he said.
"We've GOT to make noises in greater amounts!
So, open your mouth, lad! For every voice counts!"

Thus he spoke as he climbed. When they got to the top,
The lad cleared his throat and he shouted out, "YOPP!"

And that Yopp . . .
That one small, extra Yopp put it over!
Finally, at last! From that speck on that clover
Their voices were heard! They rang out clear and clean.
And the elephant smiled. "Do you see what I mean? . . .
They've proved they ARE persons, no matter how small.
And their whole world was saved by the Smallest of All!"

"How true! Yes, how true," said the big kangaroo.
"And, from now on, you know what I'm planning to do? . . .
From now on, I'm going to protect them with you!"
And the young kangaroo in her pouch said, . . .

"... ME, TOO!
From sun in the summer. From rain when it's fall-ish,
I'm going to protect them. No matter how small-ish!"